Bath Night and Hockey Sticks

Bath Night and Hockey Sticks

✦

Growing Up Canadian In The 1930s

A Novel

Robert E. Miller

iUniverse, Inc.

New York Bloomington Shanghai

Bath Night and Hockey Sticks
Growing Up Canadian In The 1930s

iUniverse books may be ordered through booksellers or by contacting:

iUniverse
1663 Liberty Drive
Bloomington, IN 47403
www.iuniverse.com
1-800-Authors (1-800-288-4677)

Because of the dynamic nature of the Internet, any Web addresses
or links contained in this book may have changed
since publication and may no longer be valid.

This is a work of fiction. All of the characters, names, incidents,
organizations, and dialogue in this novel are either the products of the
author's imagination or are used fictitiously.

ISBN: 978-0-595-43029-1 (pbk)
ISBN: 978-0-595-87371-5 (ebk)

Printed in the United States of America

Especially to my wife Betty, son Rob, daughters four, Ralph Brinsmead, and the support of family and friends past and present.

1

On this spring day in 1939, before the war had begun, I was having a party to honour my twelfth birthday—an event I did not wish to celebrate. It was also a day in which I made pocket money by becoming involved in one of Grandad Cade's most satisfying public escapades. In addition, on that same day I learned that the match between the Turnbull Tigers and the Edmonton Royals was on. Because I knew word must be out, I was up early Saturday morning finished with my chores and all set to head down to Gassing's for the latest Turnbull hockey news. Unfortunately, this Saturday, February 18th, mother had invited guests for a noontime birthday party. Consequently, she would not let me out of the house until I had taken a bath, and made myself presentable. Any other time, the scrub and tub could have taken place just before or right after Hockey Night in Canada—six o'clock Western—and here it was, nine o'clock on a Saturday morning, of all things, I was ordered to the tub.

"Ah mom can't I do it later?" I complained.

"Just go bring in the laundry tub as asked."

"Well supposing I just wash up. A sponge bath sort of?" There was more to just having a bath on Saturday morning but I could not admit it. My mind was full of 'what ifs': what if Mrs. Appleby just walked through the door and saw me in the tub. Mrs. Appleby, Fern's mother, lived next door and frequently just popped in. She was, in my mind always just popping in, she or some other neighbour lady; or maybe even Blair or somebody just walked in; what if Fern …? I did not want Fern to find me naked in a tub; although it occurred to me that, I might just not mind seeing her in a tub. The problem was, like many households of the day, there was not a bathroom in the house. In order to have a bath, a laundry tub was set down on the floor in front of the cook stove, and hot water from a boiler ladled into the tub which would already have a few buckets of cold poured into it. It was there in the kitchen or sometimes, if it was mother the tub was taken into her bedroom but that was not usually the case for kids.

"You can hook the back door," said mother with finality and seeing through my transparencies.

I got clean enough on the outside but inside there was grit and grime a plenty. Even though the ritual was usually pleasurable, this time it served mostly to further the distance already existing between mother and me.

Naturally, I protested her decision but only for the record, knowing there was only one way to gain the freedom of the outdoors and that was to capitulate for I wanted only to get myself outdoors into that balmy day. The itch was particularly strong since, until that date, there had been precious few days to celebrate. Cold, wind and snow had been the order for months. It was weather so inclement that neither Blair nor I tramped the woods searching out snowshoe hares or setting traps for weasels. Still, the winter months had been interesting. The hockey season was well under way, our School Christmas Concert was over and done, we had put on the Turnbull and District Ice Carnival and Fun Day, and now here it was hockey finals. And only recently some good days for cross country skiing with but one outing to catch a sighting of great snowy owls as well as a watch of bohemian wax wings——just two of our wintering species of birds. All in all, other than for a few bad blizzard days, winter was as usual pretty interesting in Turnbull. And this sun bright Saturday looked to be one of the best of the season.

Once out the back door, I skipped hurriedly past friends' houses not wishing the company of either male or female. Yet, I felt a trifle cowardly for slipping by unseen and not giving a wave to Fern. Fern, just one year older, a best buddy and confidante, was also a guest for the birthday not, of course, at all her fault.

"Jamie, you know you like your mother's special chiffon cake," consoled Fern, ever practical, and knowing, as I did, that the birthday was not subject to cancellation. But I wanted no further talk about being inside playing host to company whose interests lay mainly in the cake and ice cream, for that reason I detoured down the back lane.

So it was, that hours away from the party, I stood alone soaking in the sunshine, looking at miles and miles of beautiful white snows starting with the street in front of me and going beyond as far as one could see. There right before me was the inviting challenge of a waist high drift that had started right at our street and then, whipped by the wind, a magnificent expanse all the way onto main, and out beyond the village proper. Where, in bright sun, it spread across the open fields to the edge of the sky like ocean surf. Had I worn skis, I could easily have glided right to downtown where I expected to find Whizzer Jackson. Mind you, there were a few dug paths but they were little challenge or of tremendous hazard, depending on your point of view, as not every lot owner bothered to scatter ashes over their share of the front street board walk; this according to by-law. As regards to roads, the Village Council operated on the theory that the snow was bound to melt soon so near it was to spring. It was a policy not with out controversy. Generally, village shopkeepers supported the unofficial position while the housewives very much opposed, they being the ones most often having to manoeuvre the rutted walks with arms full of groceries and children in tow. The farm population was divided: some thought it a great challenge and an opportunity to show off their fanciest match of horses and sleighs and rather sensibly believing packed snow a better road bed than street cleaned down to mud and gravel. The rest just wanted to go about their business with a little more ease and a chance to ride to town in an automobile.

Actually, there had not been an automobile down Main Street since late December because most owners had long since put their vehicles up on blocks. The mayor adhered to this practise and so he, for one, was not concerned about snow-plugged streets. As long as farmers could come to town by team over the municipal roads, which the council wasn't responsible for in the first place, then it didn't much matter what the Village did in the way of snow removal. A matter of fiscal responsibility, opined the mayor, to the disgust of his detractors. Captain Jack, being one, was careful not to say anything offensive within earshot. In private, the Captain, oftimes would pull his bantam rooster like self up and full vent blast at the mayor's inadequacies. I should explain; Jack Simpson was not an actual captain of anything but for some vague reason Jack was either first named or called Captain by most everyone in the community. Young kids, like me, innocently thought back then that it was a title going with the job of rink manager.

The main reason for maintaining a semblance of politeness in his dealings with the penny-pinching mayor was because he controlled the funds for the community skating rink and Captain Jack, our long time icemaker, needed the winter job to supplement an otherwise meagre income. And in truth, here it was, the birthday hindering one more of my activities—that of helping the Captain out on Saturday.

"You'll get yourself all wet and dirty," said Mother.

Any other Saturday she would have said nothing, believing it better for me to be doing something useful "And stay out of mischief ... no wet clothes." she added as I scurried out the back door of the house.

Gassings' Mechanical and Repair was just past the rink and it was there I expected to find Whizzer and get the scoop on whether or not the Turnbull Tigers had made it to the playoffs. It would make the birthday more palatable if I could present this news to the gathering and possibly by doing so prevent Lucy Spooner from manipulating everything.

I should like it known just for the record—I realize you may think it a petty point—that Lucy Spooner was one of that kind for whom every social occasion is a personal challenge to set in order. Even mother could not forestall Lucy. Somehow, she could manage to get any party going in a direction of her making. In retrospect, she did keep things lively with a mental store of games always at the ready should the real host fail to deliver. However, she also had an unending supply of risqué jokes and stories. She could look you full in the eye and blandly ask ... "I'll bet you don't know the main parts of a stove?"

Some dupe would confidently start listing off items until she would interrupt with her stock statement ... "Oh don't be so dumb! They are lifter, leg, and poker." The sophisticates amongst us would practically roll over in laughter as the dupe invariably stammered and blushed.

While these stories were juvenile in context and quite forgettable, as eleven and twelve year olds we thought them to be pretty daring stuff. Moreover, if sometimes I was embarrassed by Lucy's stories, I confess like most of the young males of the day, I was overawed by her verbal powers and ability to talk unblushing about forbidden things.

My struggles with the drifts lasted for two blocks before I clambered out at the end of an alley on to a street, which was less snow-filled. I was actually having a pretty good time plunging over drifts and hated to have it end. As I rolled over the last major drift and belly flopped onto the street, a voice directed a call at me.

"Hey boy! You there! Come on over here," came a thin testy voice shouting out from somewhere near. I squirmed on to one side got my head up but still could not see the caller.

"Don't you got eyes?"

Finally, I saw him standing against the unpainted side of Henderson's ice shed. It was the elderly but unmistakable, cocky figure of Grandad Cade. Not my own grandfather, I hasten to assure, but that of Crazy Cade, so dubbed by less charitable members of the village.

"I'm sorry I couldn't see you in the shadow."

"No matter, you see me now. I got a job for a bright boy like you. Money in it," he added seeing my hesitation. Fact of the matter was, while I would never have spoken of him as "Crazy Cade" even amongst my friends, I, at the same time, did not want to be seen as being associated with him either.

Whatever else he might have been, Grandad Cade was no fool and was quite aware of what people thought of him. Yet none of it dissuaded him from his self-appointed civic tasks. Today, he had a new crusade and needed an errand boy. If my mother was not already sending me on one, he added. Since I found it hard to lie, when asked a direct question, I allowed that I was not doing anything in particular.

"Thought it likely. You're the Sinclair boy ain't you."

It was not a question. He was merely sizing me up by scanning me over with his piercing blue eyes. I stood respectfully awaiting his verdict. He seemed lost in thought for several moments while contemplating my being. I clearly remember how he looked on that day. Never in fashion, he wore a faded denim smock buttoned over an enormous wool sweater. His head was capped with one of those fur-lined hats complete with earflaps and his feet were shod with genuine Indian moccasins and rubbers, the kind that Easterners persist in calling galoshes.

"Sinclair ..." he mused, "so you be a cousin to young MacLean. Am I right?"

"Yes sir." I agreed, pleased he knew that Busher and I were related.

"Good Christian names—after King James, the King that seen fit to put out a proper version of the Good Book. No matter, I expect you know about that. But don't have time for that this morning. How would you like to earn a dime boy? It's honest money for honest work." I nodded agreement. He explained my mission was to find Arch Macdonald for him. "Going to teach that old humbug the Mayor a thing or two. If the Lord was into taking sinners early he would be long gone, I always say." Cade swung his walking stick in the air to emphasize the point, making me hope again that nobody I knew might see me with the old gentleman. For gentleman I knew him to be. My father told me that, even if as people said he was a touch crazy. "Now you tell Arch Macdonald I'll give him two dollars for going up and down Main Street. I want him at my place one o'clock. Tell him to get out his sleigh bells," he hollered as an after thought. I took off in search of Arch.

I figured him to be unloading a boxcar as he had mentioned the likelihood of it on Tuesday.

I found him easily enough.

"Old man Cade said that?"

I assured Arch that he had.

"Well I suppose his money's as good as the next. Don't know what the Mayor will think. But, what the heck; tell Mr. Cade I'll be there 'bout ten past one—maybe sooner. I've got to deliver and unload this lot of salt first. You be there too Jamie. Might as well have a first class seat for the show."

I took a chip of stock salt to suck on the way back. It was red as usual. I hurried back at a quick jog down the cleanest path I could find, feeling part of a juicy adventure, an enormous secret just need-ing some one to share it with.

I found the old man in his back yard busily uncovering what appeared to be nothing more than a pile of old boards and miscella-neous junk.

"Arch said he would come," I burst out rather breathlessly.

"That all he say?" I shrugged not wanting to repeat exactly what Arch did say. Cade eyed me briefly but with good humour. "Probably said I was a crazy old fool. Don't need to answer that, boy. How about earning another dime? Help me clear away this pile of snow and boards."

I pitched in not caring about the dime at all. In short order we had moved the boards and uncovered a peculiar wooden prow with some chunks of iron attached. I knew of Cade's Ark and was worried by the thought that I might be becoming involved in one of his embarrassing street preaching episodes.

"What's that?" I asked cautiously expecting some biblical object.

"That my boy is a snow plow. Made it myself and if we get it free we're going to use it to show the mayor and his no-good council just how things can get done with some honest effort and a little faith in the Lord."

After ten minutes of hard shovelling on the rest of the contraption, we dug it out. It was a crude simple rig shaped like a letter A and looked like it might just work. The prow, reinforced with iron strapping together with a hand-made bolt and a piece of chain made up the hitch. The mid-section consisted of a wooden platform piled with rocks for ballast. The entire length of the plow was no more than ten or twelve feet and about man high wide. Wide enough, Cade explained, to track a Model-T with space enough to walk beside it. I must have looked a bit dubious for Cade was quick to state that it had worked before and what's more, a whole lot of `Thomas's` were going to be quite surprised when it did so again.

"Yes sir," I agreed feeling slightly dishonest, knowing I too was a Thomas.

"Well sir, sun is sitting at about lunch time." He cast an eye at the sun and with a little dramatic flourish pulled out his gold cased watch, then snapped the lid open to confirm it. "Minute past, my timing is getting off. Happens when you get older, but then time don't mean much to me anymore. Well let's go then. Mother Cade will have soup on and homemade biscuits. You like homemade biscuits don't you?"

He didn't actually wait for a response and sort of herded me into the back porch. No mention made nor need for my mom's approval. On Saturday, meals were quite laissez-faire except for supper. I had to be home in time for supper but for the rest of the day I was on my own. I got fed if I came home or stopped at a chum's house. No phoning home because like most we did not have one. In those days if an important out of town call came for a citizen, a messenger dispatched from the phone office and a time set to take the call at the office itself. No charge made until after the call was completed.

Arch Macdonald arrived within minutes of the appointed time. He was there in the lane inspecting the plow by the time we had finished lunch. Arch did not say anything favourable or unfavourable about it. His dray and team of horses stood quietly by.

"You want me to pull it down Main Street do you?" he asked.

"Yep. And two dollars when the job is done if that's agreeable."

"Two dollars is fine. More than enough. I'm not sure I am going to earn it," responded Arch, his tone of voice just a shade sceptical.

"She'll do it, don't you go worrying about that."

"You riding along?"

"That's what the box is for," said Grandad Cade as he took a grip on the apple box that he then mounted with unexpected alacrity.

Arch eyed the man and machine for a few contemplative seconds, not wishing to see either the person or the pride of the old man injured.

"Okay Mr. Cade. I'll unhitch the team." He proceeded to grasp the double tree in one hand repositioning the Clydesdales from the dray to the plough and casually placing the lynch pin with the free hand before politely ushering Cade out of harms way; then put the team to pulling and began working the plough loose. Nothing happened at first try, even aided by Cade who busied himself with a shovel, poking and prying away at the frozen runners.

"Just hold up there Mister Cade. We'll try her one more time." Arch urged his team off to the side and Nellie, the most willing of the pair dug in and put some extra power into the pull. This time the old plough came cracking out of its icy bed even as Cade and I hollered out encouragement. Bang! It was too much encouragement.

The plough moved along all right but the bow chain tore off in the process. The whole thing settled back into the soft snow like a sinking ship.

"Well she moved a bit," said Arch trying to be positive and sparing of Cade's feelings. He need not have worried since lack of optimism was never one of Grandad Cade's failings. He immediately headed for his back porch motioning for me to come along. The inside was an organized jungle. There, in a pile, lay scores of bundled newspapers, and old magazines—all on a day when formal recycling depots were non-existent. Added to this, a box of tools, a coalscuttle, wood box, scraps of metal and wood, rags, and flattened tin cans nailed to numerous cracks in the wall. Cade poked amongst the contents of old one-quart oil cans, found a U-bolt, and took a coil of No.9 baling wire off a wall hanger. The wire, as much of the other stuff, was a hold over from farming days and kept on hand for minor emergencies and repairs.

"You can carry the tool box. But don't go banging it around. Mrs. Cade has a little nap after lunch and we don't wish to disturb her. She is not like me," he confided, "once I'm up I don't ever go lay down till its bedtime 'less I get sick. That don't happen very often either." With this little bit of history taken care of, we lugged the stuff out to the plough.

Arch volunteered to do the job. Cade raised no objection and so Arch first off cut a chunk of wire about two feet long then wound it in and around both the iron prow and a U-bolt in this way creating a temporary chain link, which, after a little testing, appeared to be good enough for the job. Myself, I could not help but think of that ancient poem which ... "For want of a nail the shoe was lost ... and on and on until it gets on to the punch line ... "... for want of a horse the War was lost."

Arch hitched the team back up and this time the plow slipped ahead as smooth as silk with the bits of ice and frozen mud shearing off the sides. Unfortunately, I noticed that while it now moved it wasn't doing much of a job of cleaning off snow.

"Looks a little rough don't it?" Cade observed. "It'll do better. Just shift a few of them rocks more up front."

Arch and I looked doubtful but we obliged. "Just like laying out ballast on a ship," he continued, "you gotta set it right or she don't settle in and do the job."

This time it worked, laying down a beautifully clean six-foot path, just as Grandad Cade said it would. Arch, a big smile on his face, swung onto the lane and back in again. "She's all right Mr. Cade."

"Yep just like I said," Cade responded, looking pleased and vindicated.

For the first block, to get the feel of things, Arch and I trotted along side on foot while the old man rode settled down on his apple box throne. Once we reached sight of Main Street, Arch stopped and then straddled the sides in a drayman's stance motioning me onto the rocks.

"Might as well ride in style. Put on a little show for the folks," said Arch then, getting into the spirit of things, he snapped the reins and set the team trotting off with their harness bells ringing.

Down Main Street we came: A King, his driver, and me Prince Jamie at his feet. The harness bells merrily heralded our arrival.

Grandad Cade waved grandly with his walking stick as if anointing his subjects. The timing was perfect, we hit main street when the majority of business owners were trudging through the snow back to their respective premises—the hired helpers: clerks, mechanics, and the like, having already taken theirs' and the employers were returning from the second shift as it were. Single owner shop keepers simply put *Gone to Lunch* signs on their doors whereas the Creamery and feed places just shut their doors after putting out an, *Open at One* sign in the shop window.

The looks we got while making our way down Main Street was worth the trip itself: Judge Whittaker, also the town's lawyer, giving us a look somewhere between indignation and distaste stumbled over the snow bound walks and tried to pretend that nothing of significance was happening. Even so, most of the citizens seemed amused and taken up with our efforts. Better sense eventually prevailed on the Judge and soon even he took to walking on the cleanly ploughed roadway.

Grandad Cade, cherishing the moment, did not even notice.

When we got as far as the Mayor's office, Cade called a halt.

"Don't want his honour to miss nothing," he confided. Then belting out in his street hardened preacher's voice, "Come on out here and listen to a citizen," he bawled, whilst cupping his hands to give more force to this verbal assault upon the door of Thomas A. Fawcett

Insurance Agent. The mayor, inside and behind closed doors, was unaware of the events outdoors.

At first, there was not a lot of coming out. Once a face, though not the Mayor's, peered over the green half-high window curtains. Then, the faded curtains parted and the Mayor himself peered out, prompting Cade to remark that the first ray of light in years had just now entered the place. The small gathered crowd laughed good-naturedly at this witticism. Seconds later, the Mayor and the unknown face, a crony, were standing holding the door open yet neither in nor out in person. The Mayor, however, took the precaution of covering his baldhead with a hat. Whether it was in response to the cold air or an act of vanity, I do not know.

"Well, well, if it isn't old Mister Cade himself. Well now, what are you up to today? Somebody doing business on Sunday again? Street light went out on your corner. What might it be this time?" the Mayor asked, hoping for some minor matter to deal with. Then an aside, "Can't get an honest day's work done around here some days. Well if you got some complaint Mr. Cade, the town's always willing to listen. Just step on down off that rig and come on in."

"Honest," roared Cade in full flower and ignoring any proffering of Olive Branches. "Don't talk to these good folks about honest. There ain't hardly a soul in this town needs enlightening about honest especially from council members."

The Mayor's face reddened but he managed to retain a little aplomb knowing that entering into a Cade debate could never make him a winner.

"Well my office is always open for opinion. Did you come here for pleasure Mr. Cade or did you have something important to say … maybe another town beautification scheme perhaps?" He got a small chuckle for his last remark, as one of Cade's last schemes was to have the town maintenance man made responsible for hanging up flower baskets on the Main Street's lampposts during the summer months. The plan got as far as a vote but killed because of the assertion that it would just be a waste of water, which after all had to be hand pumped and hauled by the barrel. Cade was, I think, often ahead of his time.

"Now you just take a look down that there street," said Cade rising from his apple box throne and pointing dramatically with his walking stick. The Mayor looked and got a good look at the freshly ploughed street, the sight of which caused his brain to stall in neutral.

Obviously, he did not know what to say. One side of Main had a six-foot wide snow free path running for two blocks. The other was rutted and full of drifts.

"That street, as any fool can plainly see, just got cleaned properly for the first time this winter. And I have to say … I have to say though it pains me some, that you and that bunch of old women running this town … you been saying it couldn't be done with out great expense. Far too much money you said. I tell you something when me and Mr. Macdonald here is done the whole street is going to get clean for the princely sum of two dollars. Two dollars. Ladies and gentlemen just two dollars! Now I'm willing to donate my machine free of charge if the village pays the team and the man. What do you say to that?"

"Well now … well now I suppose the offer's fair enough. But what if it has the same reliability of that Ark you built? Think the Village ought to take the chance?"

There were a few more chuckles from the crowd causing the mayor to think that perhaps he had swayed them, in truth, few were actually laughing, for while appreciating a little humour, they were siding with Cade despite the reminder that he had indeed once begun the building of an Ark, quoting many biblical sources for doing so. He even attempted to solicit a subscription to help pay for it. Alas, years later the incomplete Ark could still be seen landlocked and decaying on the edge of a muddy slough at the Cade home place.

"Well sir," responded Cade dramatically, "this here plough probably last at least as long as any promises the council might make."

The Mayor realizing he was losing suggested that perhaps if the machine was as good as advertised it should make another round or two. The mayor now, noticed the baling wire as well as the deteriorated condition of the rig, obviously was thinking that a break could easily occur.

"Ha!" said Cade, beginning to show a little irritation. "Don't you never mind about my plough; she'll do just fine. What we got a right to know is if this council going to do something about cleaning the streets or not."

"Here here," someone called out from the crowd, which clearly was fast getting on Cade's side of the matter.

"What about it, Tommy?" This time it was a robust male voice hollering out from the growing number of gathering citizens.

A few more voices joined in, and the Mayor knew that some sort of commitment, palatable stall, something, had to be made. Just what, he appeared not to know. Fortunately, for Mayor Fawcett, Judge Whittaker finally reached the scene and joined the Mayor on the sidewalk. He put his voice to the mayor's ear and whispered some bit of advice.

"Folks …" began the Mayor, looking quite relieved. "Folks … now I want you to know that me and my council all share your concerns and so does the Judge here but you see cleaning of the streets is not a simple matter; there are legal ramifications …" he paused, appealing to the judge to make certain he was getting it right.

"Don't you go hiding under no legal blanket," roared Cade up again onto his feet and waving his walking stick like a rapier in the direction of the mayor. "And you there Whittaker, you can also pay attention to a senior member of this town."

"It is not a town it is a village," the Judge corrected, gamely trying to side track Grandad Cade.

"Any fool knows that even an educated one," responded Cade, his anger having abated somewhat but his willingness for righteous battle still growing.

"I was just advising the Mayor that he cannot make promises just to appease a citizen's complaint. This can of course be brought up properly at the next duly convened council meeting. And, I should advise you sir that you are at this moment not within your rights to tamper with town streets."

"Why you old goat ..." Cade had lost it again and a growl as menacing as old man Schultz's bull terrier rose in his throat.

"You don't do nothin' about the streets and now you threaten a senior citizen for showing the way."

Judge Whittaker, was quite unprepared for such ferocity, and tried to sidestep this wrathful, Old Testament Prophet incarnate. Then realizing that being legally correct only seen as against the public good, he appealed to the Mayor, who was now seeking relief on the sidelines. No help there. Finally, in what he considered a diplomatic approach, the judge offered to send a man around and clean Cade's walk and got called an old goat a second time.

This was too much. The judge, eyes blazing, headed straight towards his glittery-eyed opponent who was himself poised for battle, walking stick at the ready. The mayor had the wit to catch hold of the judge.

"Alvin ... Alvin you musn't," he cajoled, using Whittaker's almost forgotten first name. "He's just a crazy old man; you mustn't take offence Alvin," he soothed.

"Crazy? Who says I'm crazy?" cried Cade. Being a little deaf, he was not certain of who said what.

Arch, who had been calmly minding the team and I suspect enjoying the fracas, decided he had best intervene and reached over to calm Cade. Unfortunately, in that same moment, a mongrel dog, yelping in terror, with old man Schultz's bull terrier at his heels in hot pursuit, fled underneath the dray in and amongst the feet of the horses. I must report here that although there was a Village by-law pertaining to dogs loose on the streets, in those days few people, if any, observed the by-law. In this case Shultz, living just off Main Sreet, never leashed his dog and so being the bully that it was, Shultz's dog naturally just set upon any dog straying near—the one exception being Jamieson's Irish terrier. During the melee that followed, the mongrel got himself tangled in Toby's traces causing the normally docile gelding to panic. The gelding took off running taking Nellie and the rig along with him at the very instant she was finishing a call of nature. "No doubt," offered Captain Jack "the horse just wanted part of the action."

At any rate, we suddenly had a crowd scattering from the runaway as the team and rig pitched straight through the onlookers. Mind you, it was not much of a runaway, only momentary exciting, with no injuries. The pair of Clydesdales ran full steam for only about a block and a half. Still, I got a scare and clung grimly, belly down, onto the rock ballast. Grandad Cade, on the other hand, smiled and waved through it all. Arch, being the teamster he was, stayed astride the plough and soon had the horses calmed down.

He then swung the team across the intersection, putting them to work cleaning the opposite side of the street on up and past the Mayor's office, leaving a snow cleared roadway. "Wide enough for man and beast," quipped Cade gleefully, as we arrived back at the point of departure. Cade, not yet through with his verbal attack, rose majestically once we stopped and pointed to the steamy pile Nellie had left on the street.

"Friends …" he hollered in the dramatic street style he had perfected over the years, "friends," he repeated, "… that there pile is a perfect example of council policy. It's all horse manure. Raises a lot of steam and stink when it's fresh up and is nothin' but an old pile when it's cold." Cade then turned his back on both the Judge and the Mayor leaving them speechless and standing awkwardly in front of the *Thomas H. Fawcett, Insurance* sign. We finished Main with Cade waving grandly at each and every citizen watching our progress. For good measure, we ploughed the side street right past the homes of both the Mayor and the Judge. Arch enjoyed the whole affair so much he refused the two dollars when it came time to settle up. Grandad Cade wouldn't hear of it.

"A deal's a deal Mr. Macdonald. You got kids ain't you?" That sort of settled it so Arch took his pay.

"Only one thing I regret," he said looking more at me than Arch. "I lost my head, shouldn't have called the Judge an old Goat ... even ... even if I think he is I shouldn't have said so." His fiery eyes fixed upon me as he spoke, "It ain't Christian boy and it was against my principles. Mind you," he paused with a twinkle in his eyes, "as a sin it was only a little one. Still it wasn't right. I attacked the man not his intentions or lack thereof. Try to remember that."

"Yes sir."

By the time we rode back and unhitched I was late for my party, and I still hadn't found out whether or not the Tigers made the play offs so thinking if I had something of value to announce when I got home maybe it would serve to distract my mom. I started back down town with Arch.

"Say young fellow shouldn't you be going in the other direction?"

I knew there was no use trying to lie about it, especially after Grandad Cade's revelations. I levelled with Arch and explained it.

2

I found out about the game in the most obvious way. I got off the dray heading not quite sure to where; stopped in my tracks and got the inspiration of the day. I asked Arch.

"That all you want to know? Word came in last night. The team is in. Whizzer Jackson told me this morning while I was making a delivery to Gassing's."

I was surprised but only at my own stupidity. So intent had I been, on escaping the birthday and, second caught up in Grandad Cade's escapade, I had not asked Arch for any information. Arch usually had the latest information on village happenings. I hasten to assure you that this was so not because he was gossipy by nature. Arch was affable and never a gossip. Rather, it was natural, almost inherent, to his business, which took him daily, excepting Sunday, to the main sources of village activity. You might say that he was a latter-day living bulletin board.

Quite elated with my newfound information, I headed off home now able to face the birthday party and thinking, that by bearing such hot news, it alone might get me off the hook for being absent. The surprise was on me. My father had already told my mother the news at lunchtime. She was not receptive to my excuses. Moreover, there wasn't anyone at the party who didn't know about it, not even Lucy Spooner. However, there was consolation to be found; because by being late, I had escaped the dreaded birthday kisses that the girls of that age thought to be so daring; most especially, I didn't have to face nor be kissed by Lucy Spooner.

Fern Appleby I wouldn't have minded; but, as Fern politely put it "Number one it's downright silly to do it in front of an audience, and two, Jamie we're buddies!" which pretty much summed up my feelings as well.

My cousin Lisa was another matter. I daydreamed about her a lot but I only saw her if she came to town and stayed at my Grandma's.

There was, however, an additional bonus for having been late. The fact that the party had started without me, also resulted in it hardly lasting once I finally arrived. Mother said very little to me in front of my soon to depart guests, a forbearance on her part for which I was grateful. My limp apologies over, we got right to eating the cake and ice cream and from there the party rather dwindled away. That meant time before supper for Blair and me to have a visit with Captain Jack. Mother did not object, happy I think, not having to deal with me further. As soon as we were out the door, I launched into the telling of my version of the snow-ploughing episode.

Next morning, Sunday, I awoke early still thinking about Saturday's happening and the exciting things to come because of the Playoffs. Just how the event would shape the days ahead in our village were delicious and heady thoughts indeed. Turnbull Tigers had made the finals. I could hardly believe it and wanted, upon waking, to immediately go down to the rink so I could talk about it. But it was, after all, Sunday and first was the obligatory attendance to Church and Sunday School. That meant there would be only an hour and a half of rink time in which to play shinny. Unless, of course, I was able to persuade my mother to delay my lunch time until twelve thirty. It being Sunday, it was wishful thinking to even consider asking, yet, young boys being what they are, I was tempted and might have done so but for the knowledge that, as forgiving as my mother was, I was still in disgrace over the birthday. I did have a thought, and that was to get to the Church early and then volunteer to ring the steeple bell. I figured I might be able to get it rung four or five minutes early and thereby move the proceedings on a little. And, because I was the first of the two persons to properly pull the bell rope, I had the say as to when to start.

There was no set time, on Sunday mornings, when one was expected to actually arrive at the rink, but it was immensely more satisfying to be there at the start and with luck be able to play for the full two hours. Sometimes Captain Jack chased us all off early if he had not flooded the ice the night before—this happened most often after a Tigers Saturday night home game. However, on this particular Sunday there was no night game to clean up after and since only general skating was scheduled we expected a full two hours of unfettered hockey pleasure. I was understandably anxious to get myself to the rink as early as possible.

Even so, as I recall, we were not allotted two full hours of play. The fact was that we were shorted fifteen minutes and to a boy, complained loudly of the unfairness of it all.

"Boys," Captain Jack ignored the complainer choosing instead to address the entire small group of players, "Boys!" once more to get everyone's attention. "Can't do it today. You see with the nice warm weather, just about the whole town will want to be skating, and ..." another pause for effect, "there will be lots of girls."

His last comment brought on a few groans, particularly from amongst the youngest players. When pressed by the more vocal voices of the motley crew of shinny players for some better reasons, the finally exasperated Captain told us flatly that whatever time we got was at his pleasure and saying no more walked away. Even as he did, there continued to be some grumbling and mild pleading; done more for effect than out of any conviction he was about to change his mind. Besides, the game had been such glorious good fun we were in quite high spirits and had no real wish to quarrel.

"Come on guys. Captain's right. Time to go," said Johnny Marks, a high school age player who finally lead us off. "Thanks for the time Captain."

"Thanks Captain Jack." Most of us echoed Johnny's words as we stepped off the ice in full knowledge the Captain did his best and we did not wish to appear ungrateful.

For, truth be known, we knew, that Captain Jack did have to give precedence and be fully prepared for a large early turnout of family skaters. Moreover, the ice schedule spelled out the allotted time for each on-ice activity. The shinny players, in practise, usually impinged upon the family skate simply because the turnout for that particular group rarely started before one-o'clock. Even so, if but two young women turned up to skate, the practise was over—family skates meant just that: girls and women. If there were no females then hockey sticks abounded. Consequently, the shinny players never ceased lobbying the Captain for extra ice time. This, in spite of the fact that the schedules were strictly adhered to; having scheduled hockey practises for Junior and Intermediate men's teams at times allotted on Tuesdays and Thursdays; namely from nine p.m. to ten-thirty p.m. Midgets and Pee Wees practised after school from four to five and five to six Mondays and Wednesdays. Since shinny players usually were members of organized teams, they as a group, had little to complain about. Naturally, actual games always took ice time precedence, especially on Saturday afternoons when some of the really big games were scheduled for the Tigers.

Our shinny games were played continuously over the two hour time period: and teams were chosen initially on a more or less "equal sides" basis regardless of age and remained that way until it was felt that the scores had become too lopsided and the fun gone out of it. Late arrivals simply joined whichever side seemed in need of bolstering at the moment. No attention paid to actual numbers per side or age, as I have already stated. The game could not start before eleven a.m.—this by convention, and arrived at through a consensus of local clergymen and informal approval of the village council. Nothing was put on the books in the way of a by-law. Over time, both this unofficial constraint and the Sunday morning shinny game itself disappeared.

Captain Jack, knowing the lot of us were quite aware of the arrangement, just kept walking toward the gate and held it open as we filed off the ice. The matter settled, we grumbled no more, took off our skates, realizing in the moment, that we were hungry, that lunch would be waiting, and so dispersed happily for home. Personally, I was not particularly unhappy about losing ice time because it was a very warm day even for February. Moreover, the ice had been slow and I had a hankering to go rabbit hunting and figured it was a good day to borrow a rifle from my cousin Busher MacLean who had often told me I was welcome to use his rifle anytime he himself was not going to use it. Busher, who was nineteen, lived across town and was on the team. Turk McKenzie, the coach had instructed all his players to get in a little extra skating even though there would be no practise on Sunday. Busher also had a girl friend who liked to skate so he willingly relinquished his single shot Remington. My Dad Okayed the hunt because I was going with Blair who was dependable and also six months older than I was. My mother always fussed about it but bowed to this largely masculine pursuit. In truth, she rarely tried to talk me out of it but I knew she was happier when I did not go. Often she reminded me of the time Georgia Jensen and his brother had the accident. Georgia was shot through his own carelessness whilst crawling under a fence. My cousin, who was the first to take me hunting, always impressed gun safety upon me. Indeed had he thought me in any way irresponsible he would have never offered to lend me his rifle. Busher was that way about everything and was a levelheaded rock-solid defenseman. I heard Whizzer Jackson say so one time. Busher, not just, because he was my cousin, had the speed and stamina to make the Pros, everybody said so and even opposing teams grudgingly admitted his talents. The word was that if some of the bigger teams had had a Busher MacLean or a Whizzer Jackson they too probably would have made it as far as the Provincials. I was pretty proud to be on good terms with Busher as you can well imagine.

Blair met me just after one o'clock, and because the snow lay deep in the fields around we chose to go on skis. We had the single toe strap kind made out of pine; cheap to buy and wide bladed enough to carry your weight over unpacked snow. We had no poles and hung the twenty-two rifles over our shoulders. We carried them using leather holding straps that served the dual purpose of being both a useful carrying sling and a steadying device for aiming the rifle in the upright position. This way there was no need to flop down upon the snow banks when it came time to fire.

We were soon gliding along using a kind of glide-shuffle technique, which we had mastered.

The snow was crusted in most places providing ample support for our modest weights. We passed over the snow with little effort greatly aided by a good coat of O'Cedar paste floor wax on mine and, if memory serves, I think Blair's mom used 'Johnson's for her floors so that is what he likely used on that day. As I said, the temperature was just above the freezing point and ideal for skiing. I remember keeping my wool jacket tied to my waist for most of the day and having the earflaps on my leather helmet fastened on top. If lately, you have watched any movies with vintage airplanes in northern settings you will know the kind of winter headgear I am talking about. Not the ones Mounties are usually shown wearing, but rather the pilot and motorbike type. It occurs to me that the above freezing temperature I mentioned was actually just around 32° Fahrenheit and just below 0° Celsius—a term back in 1939 most likely only to be found in use in science labs and the like. Be that as it may, the outside temperature made for a very comfortable day to be outdoors. No wind to speak of, the sun shining brightly upon the snow reminding the world that winter's grip was fast fading. Valentine's Day was over and we only had to await the verdict of the ground hogs, although for the life of me I don't ever remember any reports of one arousing itself from its torpid state and poking its nose out to check the sun—not in my part of the world at any rate.

About forty-five minutes out, we spotted our first Jackrabbit and within seconds another one. We were by this time on the western side of Riley's slough in a grassy area stretching along for about a half mile and edging into cropland. There, the rabbits had good winter cover and food supply as well as cover within willow clumps growing here and there along the strip. Blair, a bit anxious, fired too quickly and from too far away for the kind of rifle we had. Predictably, the Jacks shot off in high gear and with great bounding leaps were soon way out of range. The miss meant we would have to tail them for a quarter mile or so and hope to get another shot if by that time they had forgotten about us or alternately forget about the Jack rabbits entirely and go after their smaller cousins; ones we called Bush rabbits because they stayed in the wooded areas and smaller meadows. Of course if you care to be technical about it neither of the two rabbit species we were chasing after were real rabbits; in the first place they were and are Hares but not being an expert in the matter I wouldn't care to speculate as to why one or the other is or isn't.

We didn't rush our pursuit, knowing that the Jackrabbits would only run so far before stopping and checking on the chasers. If not pursued, they would then carry on with their business. They did stop so we perched ourselves on a couple of large rocks, sitting well above the snow line, and discussed which way we would go. In the end, at my suggestion, we turned to the woods and left the Jackrabbits for another day. I actually preferred the woods in winter to the open because without leaves and undergrowth it opened up a world full of different creatures their sign or themselves more easily seen in their winter habitat. Vole, mouse and weasel tracks were imprinted in the snow. All were creatures harder to locate in summer and rabbit tracks were everywhere, which is why we had come to that place. The rabbits perceived our presence at once, for while we knew they were about, we had yet to spot any in the first twenty minutes of skiing along a deer's path. We did encounter one brush partridge, which was another misnomer because the bird was not a partridge at all but actually a ruffed grouse. We also got close to a porcupine balanced on the upper branch of a stout willow tree. We gave it a wide berth and did not shoot at it, as it was not the kind of game you took home; also, we adhered to the folk wisdom that said you could always kill a porcupine for food if you ever got lost in the woods. Coyotes, we knew, frequently took advantage of the porcupine's slow nature by meeting them face to face and quickly flipping them over on their backs to get at their soft unprotected bellies. I only saw a porcupine carcass once that obviously had meet its demise in this way.

On the way back home, sans rabbits, we talked about the game and wondered if our fathers would give us the necessary twenty-five cents admission. Alternatively, we would have to earn the money by seeking out Captain Jack for some kind of job. We knew that ice scraping was out as it was a job given to older and stronger boys on occasions like the coming championship game. There was no pay involved, just privileges and there was always a waiting list. Blair had just turned sixteen and even though he was strong on his skates and reliable, this time the Captain had elected to hire fat Paddy Jackson. Blair, disappointed at not being hired, would have to come up with the fifty cents. I confess too, although a little shamefaced, that we never did call him other than Fats. The Captain had a sense of duty to guide those who lacked much parenting and, in his eyes needed someone to steer them along. So, much like a boson's mate, the Captain worried over his "boys" cajoling, scolding, and punishing in equal amounts. If you did not turn up for a job, the Captain did not simply ignore you, he found you out, and you had to answer for it. He may have given up on some but it was not in his nature to do so. I should think it would have to have been a very hard case if he did.

"Captain Jack is sure to hire you this time. It's too important He can't rely on just any body," I reasoned. "Then again he might give the job to Fats." The latter idea did not sit well with either of us. We did not like Paddy Jackson for a number of reasons none of them having to do with him being overweight. One of our sometimes friends, Walter Boker was equally obese but Walter was an OK kind of guy.

Paddy in our eyes was not. Our past involvement, albeit one year before, still rankled so we rarely talked about it.

Now and again on a bright day especially in late winter, the circumstances of that foolish venture did come back and momentarily distract my thinking as it did on this day. I said nothing about it and instead broached the question as to whether or not we were likely to get one of the jobs instead of Fats Jackson.

"All kinds of guys will be looking for those jobs," Blair responded knowing that the Captain had his own set of rules about whose turn it was.

These were tenets of sorts which gave consideration as much as to whom was most in need and the like, which I suppose is why he got so much respect from the youth of the village. Even though the Captain had served in the Navy, my Father said he was only an ordinary seaman and just why he was called Captain, no one quite knew. If the title was bestowed in jest, as I suspect, none of the youth in the Turnbull took it in that way. One thing that neither Blair nor I was willing to admit openly was the considerable prestige attached to getting a rink job. It was something hard to explain to an outsider but one, which overrode the question of mere money.

Even though we talked mostly of monetary advantages, what we both knew, but did not talk about in any direct way, was the fact that paying your twenty five or fifty cent ticket did not allow you to get anywhere near the players but working the rink did. You see rink rats—the term itself was not used in those days at least not at our rink—were allowed to hang in team dressing rooms. There you could get warm; take a drink from the galvanized water pail, which you, as a helper, were charged with keeping full. And because it was hard fresh water, it both made good ice and thirst-quenching drinking water.

The dressing rooms were not much, perhaps twelve by sixteen in size, a high screened window, an old Quebec Heater—top loaded round and efficient—with a grimy single Mazda lamp hanging from the ceiling to provide light, and graffiti of a generally humorous and innocent sort gracing the shiplapped walls. Captain Jack promptly removed any cuss words.

"Well now you just had to go and break the rules, leaving me no choice but to give you a week's holiday," he would say.

A week's holiday meant being barred for a week not just from skating but even entering the rink. Only the very careless or foolish risk takers amongst us ever got the full week banishment.

Neither Blair nor I ever merited such treatment so we got the jobs. His was to scrape ice between periods and help with a quick barrel flooding after the second period weather permitting and for important Junior and Intermediate games. My task was to keep a supply of wood available for the heater and fresh water for each team room. It fell to me this time because an older boy, Butch Baker, felt it was his turn to be barrel filler. Filling barrels deemed to be a notch higher in the pecking order. It was because this allowed you to run the pump. This mechanical wonder consisted of a belt driven pump jack and a one-cylinder gas engine, that putt-putted along at a steady and easy pace once you got it going. The starting of it required agility and muscle. The main trick in the starting was to avoid getting a kickback. "Many an arm has been broken by not paying attention," Captain Jack asserted each time he started it himself and had an audience. It looked easy to do. All that was required was to grab hold of a flip-out handle, pin the flywheel around until the engine caught and then let go. Trouble was that if the gas and air mixture were incorrect the engine would back fire causing a sudden and violent reversal of the flywheel.

"Okay now Jamie this is what you are going to do." Captain Jack coaxed as he gave me instructions on how to start the thing. "Now I don't want to go breaking your arm." He looked up reassuringly as he prepared to demonstrate.

"Yes sir, Captain I'm paying attention."

"Good Lad, that's what I like about you Jamie. Now, you're a little light to tackle equipment this big, but you'll soon grow into it so I want you to be prepared when you've put a little heft into your body."

I was quite aware of this potential for arm breaking and was not anxious to test my somewhat slight frame against it; even so, Captain Jack coaxed me into turning the wheel half way round and then letting go to give me a notion of the force that was exerted. He had prudently not turned on the fuel valve just to insure that it would not fire. I confess to being nervous because Butch Baker had once convinced me to hang on to the wire leading to the magneto "Just to feel a little tingle" as he put it and howling with laughter as I got the full voltage—not life threatening but large enough to imagine it. I had been chary of the engine ever since. Nevertheless, despite my fears I put my body and arm into turning the engine over, as instructed. And, just as he said, the wheel revolved back with some noticeable force but not enough to get hurt on. I was quite pleased with this small achievement and thought that someday I could start it.

Actually, when it came to knowing about engines and machines in general, no one in town could match Doc Rafferty. He had an extraordinary mechanical mind and always had time to show off his latest device or to explain some latest scientific theory, which he had gleaned from a collection of popular journals.

We talked a bit about Rafferty, Blair and I, on that day because we both acknowledged that while our hero Whizzer Jackson, always had time to say a friendly word, we had come to understand that he was not a fountain of information in the way that Doc Rafferty was. Whizzer knew hockey. On the ice, he was a master and there was no one better.

Off the ice, we did not really know what he thought about. Our conversation about these two very disparate men did not last long because by this time both of us were hungry and growing weary from difficult skiing over softening wet snow. And, because the wax had worn off from the bottoms of our skis, our easy glide had turned into a trudge.

Despite the slow going, as we headed home, and continued to chatter on about skinning and tanning rabbit skins, and a host of imagined items we could make from the hides. In truth, neither of us had ever actually accomplished any of these tasks, nor did we have mothers willing to cook a rabbit even if we had bagged one. Aunt Polly, who lived in another town, was a possibility; once having told me that she would do it should I ever actually bring one home, and, if she happened to be around. I was content to think that one of these times it would happen if not actually today then maybe tomorrow.

We were better than half way home when the two Jacks we had been tailing earlier again made an appearance. They had followed their customary territorial circuit and we had dawdled long enough to give them time to do so. We spotted them near an old and abandoned line fence, which held enough snow each year to encourage a hedge like growth of brush and grasses. We stopped and watched as they approached still out of range.

"What do you think Blair?" The question was redundant for we both knew that they would soon spot us and even though we might get off a long-range shot, it would mean once again playing the game of follow and stop—a game the Jacks always won with us. My cousin Busher was an exception to this game; he could always get a Jack if he put his mind to it, but they had been scarce that year and he was not wont to hunt any wild creature if they were in low numbers. A chance shot wasn't worth the time. So we did a John Rafferty instead. He served as a sniper in WWI and was decorated for his actions. Rafferty was fond of reciting old saws such as "retreating and living to fight another day". This saying was only one of several, which he was fond of repeating. We wanted to quit the hunt so we used that saying as the clincher. Rafferty, I should add, was the other person who could always shoot a rabbit if he wished.

As I have explained, we had an affinity to Rafferty because, although he was one of those "high toned" Englishmen who Captain Jack liked to rail about, he was also affable and talented. He had come to live in our village quite before I was born and, so my father said, did little with his life before the war. He was a Remittance Man and had enough income sent each month from England to allow him to live in a small cottage and generally be simply a man about town with time for drinks, parties, sports, literary quotes and not much else. After the war he came back changed and because he now had a modest soldiers pension to add to the mysterious monthly cheque he had opened up a shop.

Raffertys, was to me the most intriguing shop in town. To start, it was graced with the most artistic sign in town. It consisted of a wrought iron brace—which the owner had himself made—holding a wooden English Pub Style sign out over the sidewalk. John Rafferty had somehow acquired a sign maker's hand. Consequently, he first painted both sides in royal blue before lettering in gold and scarlet; adding fancy curling borders and what we all took to be his family crest centered at the top. The only thing that could possibly have been included was, *By Appointment to HRH*. While it had been up for some time and fading slightly, it was still a thing to be admired. When I became old enough to take my skates for sharpening to his shop, I always stopped to admire it before entering the premises. Several aspects of his shop's business were not advertised on the sign—certain services: the likes of, *Electrical Gun and Bike Repair* and *Battery Service*. Even so, he just as carefully painted these and others on the shop windows still not covering his range of interests. Moreover, there was yet another facet to John Rafferty that was indeed an asset in our young eyes, he was a member of the Hockey Committee and although I had never heard of him having every played the game he sometimes served as manager of our Pee Wee Hockey team. A willing workhorse who somehow always managed to get what ever it was we were short of, even transportation, for our occasional out of town games.

3

Back to school Monday, I got all of the playoff details. Every kid in the class knew more than I did. That I didn't have the facts was more than a little deflating, considering my efforts of the previous two days. The Turnbull Tigers would play a best of two, total score game—a rather odd but not unusual arrangement agreed to principally because money was tight and travel not easy. The playoff opponents were the Edmonton Royals, of the Urban Junior "C" city league; and the Turnbull Tigers, the 1939 rural challengers. I should add that this was the second time in a mere five-year span that the Tigers had made it that far. Unfortunately, no rural team had actually unseated a city championship team in recent memory, although there had been some near misses. Local wisdom had it that the current team had the best chance ever, thus generating considerable excitement and expectation amongst the local populace. The first game in the series was to be held Saturday afternoon in Turnbull, visiting team arriving on the six o'clock passenger running from Edmonton to Calgary stopping at points in between. The after game banquet was to be held at six o'clock Saturday evening; the Royals delaying their return to Edmonton until Sunday—this being an arrangement with the CNR, allowing the team to catch the non-stop Sunday Flyer back to Edmonton.

As soon as school was out, I hurried down to see Captain Jack for more details about this very exciting event and of course, hoping to be first in line for one of the paying jobs that were sure to occur because of the playoffs.

"She'll take two floodings at least, one cold one hot," he confided, when I found him making some repairs to the water pump belt. "If his worship the major and those penny pinching councillors of his would spend a few cents on equipment ..." he took the moment as an opportunity to relight his pipe even as he spoke, "... I wouldn't have to keep repairing this poor old belt." He grumbled away between puffs on the pipe about both the condition of his equipment, and the inadequacies of town councillors who employed him.

I would nod in silent sympathy as he carried on with his monologue but I always suspected that had Captain Jack been given all new equipment he would have still grumbled and, in truth, I believe he took a great deal of satisfaction in making things work that lesser mortals consigned to the scrap heap.

Captain Jack as I have mentioned, was getting on in years and so only worked this one seasonal job to supplement his pension. His spring to fall months were devoted to gardening, wood cutting, and assorted private pursuits all of which he was equally meticulous and fussy about. Why he was called Captain, no one of my acquaintance could say with certainty. And, as my father had said, Captain Jack had only an ordinary seaman's ranking, obtained about the time of the Boer war; seemingly, this was the extent of his naval and military service. Aside from that, he had come west from Ontario, as a young man, finding work doing odd jobs and chores about the country while homesteading a quarter section. Curiously, since he talked of everything else in his life, he rarely mentioned his farming days except in occasional off-hand allusions to some skill or another that he had learned during this period of his life, but these references were never specific as to time and place. All I really knew about him was that everyone in town younger in age than my father always referred to him and addressed him as Captain Jack. Only when some formality warranted it he might be addressed as Mr. Simpson. He was, during the time of my childhood and youth, a local institution unto himself; story teller, philosopher, forthright open man who smoked nothing but Old Chum in his thrice daily pipe. He was quite outspoken without fear of being politically incorrect. He just spoke his mind although mindful, at times, to the wishes of those who hired him.

Even so, he was respected if not loved by most of the kids in town for his outspokenness. According to Arch, he was among the most astute of a village full of slightly eccentric older males who inhabited the place during their retirement years. Still, if one is comparing eccentrics, he was not the intellectual equal of Doc Rafferty who was neither retired nor a Doctor of any kind but easily qualified as Turnbull's most inventive eccentric citizen and, in my view, its most interesting, if perhaps less of the lovable curmudgeon which characterized the Captain. Both had English antecedents but differed in a number of respects. Doc being a man without a wife or children whereas the Captain had one grown-up son living elsewhere and a wife who was a quiet gentle person. She was decidedly the obverse side of the Simpson. She seemed perpetually fascinated by her husband and his activities; yet, did not hesitate to scold him for his more intemperate vocalizing—usually having to do with the local civic authorities. His surprisingly meek response to this would oftimes be, "Well you know it's the truth even if everybody else in town is afraid to say it."

"Now John," she would chide, "you mustn't go on like that. Jamie will think you show no respect." Then her head would rise up momentarily while doing some bit of needlework, her hand not missing a stitch, her voice soft and moderate. The Captain was particularly prone to making sweeping, critical comments directed at the practices of the Mayor and those councillors. Yet, once these verbal darts were delivered, he would always defer to Mrs. Simpson; only later, and in private, would he explain that, "Mrs. Simpson, good woman that she is, is far too willing to believe in any scoundrel once they got voted into office. Women don't understand politics and politicians," he would confide.

I was, as I had hoped, the first there to ask for the job.

"Well now Jamie I had been thinking I should offer it to Paddy Jackson. You know the lad needs some responsibility. Make him grow up. You understand?"

I did, but I still harboured great dislike for one Paddy Jackson; a fact I tried to hide from Captain Jack but I am sure I never succeeded.

Paddy was not popular amongst his fellows and the Captain probably assumed I took my cue from others. There was more to it than that.

On another Sunday, much like the day I broached the subject of a job, Blair and I had been wandering about town rather aimlessly, not even a shinny game to occupy our time, when we chanced upon Paddy Jackson. Paddy had a secret, which he wanted to share with somebody. He convinced us to follow him down a back-lane behind Engelmann's Harness and Shoe Repair; there we clambered into an empty sleigh box sitting behind and positioned near the back window of Darla's Hair Dressing Parlour.

Paddy's secret. He claimed if we hung around for a half hour at most we would catch Mr. P. Driscoll sneaking into the shop from the back alley. This was exciting and scandalous, especially on a Sunday; a truly juicy and exciting prospect in our juvenile minds.

"What do you suppose they are doing in there?" I asked in all innocence, before Blair, looking uncomfortable over my question, could jab a shut-up elbow into my ribs. Paddy did not bother to keep the scorn out of his voice.

"It means they're probably screwing around, dummy!"

"Well, I mean how does he get away with it?" I replied trying to sound sophisticated in these matters.

"Ah he probably makes up some story about having to do the books or checking up on bodies and stuff."

Paddy's was an explanation that eliminated all doubt. It seemed perfectly plausible, to Blair and me that an undertaker would have to check up on bodies even if on a Sunday; the fact that there were no bodies in the funeral parlour at the time going unnoticed. Paddy, being one of those assertive types whose manner lends credence to their words, put forth some unassailable logic to it, which upon sober reflection, would not have held water. Even so, doing 'it' on Sunday seemed beyond the pale to me. I was, as I have said, rather innocent, full of that Sunday school morality that included working on Sunday as being just short of a venial sin. It was all right to be obliging when circumstances warranted it, such as when, our neighbour—owning

Burton's Hardware—would open up the store after Church service of course—to obtain some item for a local farmer. Both he and the farmer took great pains to let any watch dog citizen know that the going was only because of some real or contrived emergency. I remember that old man Smithens seemed to have an almost-urgent need for an extra bolt or box of nails on Sunday. "He just remembered ... and it would, of course, save an unnecessary trip to town on Monday." While Burton never complained outright, he frequently found an excuse to be absent from home just before noon, when Smithens would be driving by after the ten-thirty service he attended. Burton didn't actually mind helping any of the farmers out but found it hard to be charitable with Smithens who not only took advantage of his benevolent nature, he justified his request quoting some biblical passage, lending excuse for violating the Lord's Day Act.

At any rate, there we were, on a Sunday afternoon, waiting to catch P. Driscoll committing some sinful act. Right on schedule, P. Driscoll did turn up .We could hardly breathe as he passed close by the wagon in which we were hiding. After a decent interval, in Paddy's judgment, we climbed quietly out of the wagon box and snuck up to the window of Darla's for a peek. I began to get quite worried at this point. In the first instance, I didn't think this was quite the right thing to do and was bothered as much by the fact that I was too chicken to say so. The other thing was that we were all three nervously thinking we might get caught.

"This is what we do," began Paddy, "Blair and me go in behind the shop and Jamie here goes to the front door. Simple as that."

"Wait a minute," I cried, "how come I go to the front by myself?"

"Simple. Darla likes you and your Grandma goes to Darla's just about every week. Me or Blair go to the front she's going to be suspicious."

"Of what?" I asked.

"Well ... she just is. Trust me." Paddy adopted a worldly air and looked to Blair for support. Blair, never quick-on-his feet in matters like this, couldn't come up with anything substantive. Although I felt it was both a risky and foolhardy escapade, somehow I could not bring myself to just walk away from it. So, the big idea was for me to go to the front door of the shop, peddle some cock-and-bull story about checking up on my Gamma's hair appointment. She did have, in fact, a regular Friday visit and how Paddy managed to know about it, I just didn't know, making me even further vulnerable to the scheme.

"Well just what is it I am supposed to say?"

"Kid you're smart. You'll think of the right stuff."

"What do you think Blair?" I appealed.

"Well, I dunno exactly." Blair dug his toe into the ground searching for some inspiration. "But I think Jamie is going to do the hardest part and he is the youngest and all."

"Exactly!" exclaimed Paddy.

"Dunno if something goes wrong he'll get all the blame." Blair too was now clearly looking for an out but also wanted to escape the scorn of Paddy, who was thirteen giving him some status because he was a few months older than either of us.

None of this spurious tale was to my liking and, as I said, Paddy being thirteen at the time, and us then being only twelve and eleven respectively, he won the argument. Blair pursued the matter a touch further hoping some how to escape Paddy's verbal scorn; also knowing full well that Paddy would go around telling everybody that we were a pair of wimps if we didn't go along. I think too, we thought that there might be another out: Figuring, if we got caught, we might safely claim Paddy put us up to it. Still, it was all a very school boyish prank which, even with misgivings, was of a kind we couldn't quite resist .The object of it all was to try and catch P. Driscoll in some sort of compromising situation. And, never thinking of the embarrassment it might cause Miss Darla who we rather liked. Fern, to whom I could confess almost anything, had just one word to describe the escapade.

"Dumb!" was all she said, "How could you be so dumb?" Well, all I could say was that it seemed exciting and fairly harmless at the time, you know nothing criminal or destructive just mischievous I guess you might call it; although, I confess it lurks uncomfortably in the recesses of my mind notwithstanding some of its comic aspects.

Miss Darla answered the door as scripted, she had on a rather loose chenille robe, wore bright lipstick and had her reddish tinted hair worn in an upsweep—I think it is what they called the style at the time. I very nervously gave my little spiel.

"Hi ... Yes?"

"Well ... uhm."

"Yes Jamie, what is it you want?"

"Well nothing really. I ... uhm was just wondering when Grandma's hair appointment is?"

"You do?" Miss Darla looked incredulously then, after a moment's hesitation, she opened the door and invited me in. I have felt forever a Judas for having gotten that far with the ruse. It was pretty much a lie and I didn't like myself for doing it even if I did not like P. Driscoll. None of us did but that of itself is a rather limp excuse. So I stood there living out this lie and just wanting to excuse myself and get out as quickly as possible. I almost made it when, sure enough, Grandma's appointment was found to be in order as had been carefully noted in Miss Darla's appointment book.

Miss Darla looked me square in the eye her voice was soft and gentle. "Jamie you didn't come to ask me about your Grandma. Why don't you just tell me why you really came? Someone put you up to this didn't they?"

My stammering around the questions pretty well shot any legitimacy it may have appeared I had. I was spared further embarrassment by the back room sounds of Paddy and Blair pounding on the back door, Paddy claiming that they had tried the front and gotten no answer. Miss Darla's eyes took on a startled appearance wondering, I suppose, if the voices were those of men or boys. Paddy's had darkened at this stage of early adolescence and, as I mentioned, was older than either Blair or myself. I felt foolish and remorseful. Miss Darla ushered me into the back room where P. Driscoll, his face contorted in an indescribable display of anger stood shaking a fist at a now terrified Paddy and Blair.

"Sit down there!" he ordered, pointing to three kitchen chairs. One of which he lifted over his head and then set down in one bare-armed motion as he was shirtless. He cuffed Paddy onto it with his other arm.

Paddy, trembling at the lip and with fear in his voice started to whine, figuring that a lot of noise would get him off the hook. At first, he tried to bluff his way out of matters but was cut short by an angry P. Driscoll who was growing more livid by the moment. He had as, I remember, an altogether big set of arm muscles not apparent underneath the shirt and suit he usually wore. Paddy, the wimp, tried to suggest that it was all the fault of Blair and me. P. Driscoll didn't even entertain the thought and Paddy eventually shut up. Miss Darla, while holding herself rigidly together, made a few compassionate noises and P. Driscoll calmed down enough to now consider some devious form of punishment or chastisement—we were never certain as to which it was going to be.

"You will see young gentlemen that I do not have either shirt or jacket on. That is because I had the great misfortune to spill some embalming fluid upon my person. It is deadly!" He paused for a little dramatic effect and went on, "It is why we use it in our trade and only on the dead. For the living, it burns and disintegrates the skin. To prevent this from happening, I hastened over here to Miss Darla's for some Camphor Ice, which as you well know, counteracts burns. Does it not?" We shook our heads vigorously in agreement. "You may ask your mothers about camphor ice. You may not however, and I repeat you may not utter one word about my presence here which might well be misunderstood in the community."

We nodded vigorously in agreement wishing ferverently to be in P. Driscoll's good books; by this time, we were beginning to believe we were somehow going to escape with only a little lecture. This well of optimism disappeared when he put his shirt, tie, and jacket back on—the embalming fluid stains somehow or other having disappeared—Camphor Ice I guess. P. Driscoll then announced that he would be taking us one at a time next door to his embalming parlour for a little demonstration. He motioned for Paddy to be first. Paddy is forever etched into my memory bank. He was all blubber and hanging onto the chair for dear life, the most frightened look upon his face that I have ever witnessed on a thirteen year old.

P. Driscoll stood in silence for several very long minutes before speaking. "Very well then, perhaps there is no need for a demonstration. Let me just say that had you been a mature person I would have been perfectly justified in shooting at you for attempting to break in—at that moment we thoroughly believed this statement from P. Driscoll—I might easily have mistaken you for thieves or thugs of some sort. Miss Darla, I know does have a small rifle and I shall instruct her in its use if I or some other gentlemen does not happen to be here to protect her. You do understand what could happen … gentlemen?" We continued to nod vigorously readily agreeing to P. Driscoll's every suggestion. Drowning men pulled from the waters could not have been more grateful; when he finished his monologue, finally he opened up the back door and ushered us out.

Blair and I never ever talked about that day. Our lips were sealed and if it was not for the fact that P. Driscoll has been long since dead—natural causes, I have been told—I would not be telling of it now.

4

My father went to the organizational meeting, which decided how local clubs and volunteer groups would best contribute to the success of the one play-off game being held in Turnbull itself. Even though the two game series format had already been set by the governing bodies—The Provincial Amateur Association and the Central Alberta League—the two finalists did have some input relating mostly to start times and a say about a possible total goals deciding factor in case of a two game draw. The game officials, although chosen by the respective league officers, could be challenged by either team. In addition, each team was allowed to choose up to three players from any other league team if they thought it could bolster their chances of winning. Edmonton was not expected to pick up any extra players unless something unforeseen occurred. And, in truth, there was some discussion as to whether or not the Tigers would follow suit. The local debate centered on two major points.

One, the business community took the stand that it would boost local business if they chose a player from each of the communities closest to Turnbull. Jack Fisher, of Fisher's Groceries and Dry Goods, led the group pushing to have one player from each of Grassy Pond district, and one from either the Duke or Creek Side districts, with possibly a third enlisted from the Clear Sky Bush Bullies. Carl Gassing, normally fairly neutral on the subject, raised an objection to the latter, stating that folks from out that way didn't generally shop in Turnbull. Lee, of Chang's Chinese, and Lars Jensen, who owned the local Creamery, backed coach Macdonald who simply wanted three of the best, where ever they were from, if, and only if, their acquisition would add to the chances of winning.

Mr. Fisher assured that he too wanted the best, but considering the track record of rural entries, it was unlikely that they would beat out the Edmonton team—added players or no. In the end, the Committee agreed to leave the matter up to the team and manager with the suggestion, for the record and not binding, that the coach attempts first to strengthen the Tigers with players from the aforementioned district teams. Charlie Sayers, our local editor, agreed to write an item pointing out these matters in the next issue of the paper. In the end, Carl Gassing's view brought about the agreement, largely because he was both team manager and Whizzer Jackson's employer. This arrangement, which he had made, ensured Whizzer's stay in Turnbull. Everyone agreed that without Whizzer the chances of the Tigers gaining the play-off would have been mighty slim.

The decision to hold an afternoon game didn't bring much debate, for as Mr. Fisher said, but was not quoted directly in the news paper account, "It stands to reason that folks are going to do a little shopping for supplies after the game if it gets held during the day." Adding, "It wouldn't hurt the livery business either." He was referring to, of course, the fact that Carl Gassing ran a small livery stable service as well as a mechanical repair shop and if people came from as far away as Clear Sky, however unlikely, that wouldn't hurt the business either. An agreement reached over the choice of three extra players as well as the start time for the game once settled; the committee then went on to discuss details of other matters pertaining to the hosting of Game One. Next item dealt with was the problem of how and where to billet members of the Edmonton team, there being only a few rooms available at the town's only remaining hotel. The eleven room Imperial hotel. Two rooms had permanent residents: In one resided Jasper Woverton who lived at the hotel and ran a small men's barbershop in one of the anterooms, in the other, old Mr. Jepson who seemed to help about the place doing exactly what I am not certain. Although, it is possible he may have been clerking. There was also a suite of rooms for August Schmall and his wife, plus a bar and small restaurant. August was particularly anxious to co-operate because his son Joe played second string forward; moreover, the hotel, in which he stayed, put up an annual trophy for team MVP. Before that, a trophy had been donated by the Royal Rose Hotel—apparently a grander structure, at least in memory if not in fact. Unfortunately, it burned to the ground one cold December night, and was not rebuilt. This sequence of events resulted in a shortage of available hotel rooms in Turnbull. The 1930's depression, having hit our town about the time of the fire, might also explain why it was not re-built. Of course, a few sceptics suggested that the fire was most likely an insurance scam. However, no one had been able to prove it and after a three-month stall the insurance companies paid up; whereupon, the hotel owner settled a few local bills and promptly left town causing an even greater amount of talk amongst the Village's more suspiciously minded citizens. In fairness, my father always maintained that the owner might well have rebuilt in better times. Since he had not, a committee was now struck for the billeting of the visiting team members. My father became head of this group. A second needed group, The Banquet committee, was simply given over to the Women's Institute because they were non-denominational and had the advantage of having Lily Tompkins and Mrs. Devco as their social organizers; and everyone knew that these two ladies were, the 'best-in-town', when it came to catering.

The final item on the agenda gave rise to considerable heated discussion over how or if they should pressure the Municipality into contributing money for the play-off or, failing that, supporting the Village's efforts in some other substantial way. Specifically, the councillors hoped to convince the Municipal council that it should do some road clearing; hopefully right into Turnbull and down Main Street. It was presumed, that unless another major storm hit the motorcade, it would then be able to navigate the municipal roadways given some snow clearing at the major trouble spots. The worst part of the route was a half mile stretch just north of the Village and running pretty much north to south through an open pasture, where considerable drifting of snow usually took place along the fence line and a further stretch of unimproved highway.

Unfortunately, the Edmonton team was not willing to risk traveling the country roads and had sent word that their first transportation choice would be the passenger train. This took away what little leverage the Hockey Committee thought it might have had in its efforts to influence the Municipality. The Committee now had a dilemma. They had to choose from two unsatisfactory methods for getting our boys to Edmonton. One, raise sufficient funds to purchase train fares for the team or two, find automobile owners willing to risk driving the always nearly impassable roadways. My father confided that the committee was hoping the Royals would elect to travel by automobile contingent on the roads being ploughed, even if just a standby plow was made available.

The Committee's announced position was that a motorcade was the best and most affordable choice. Needless to say the Municipal officials, having got wind of the Edmonton decision, happily decided to do nothing; consequently, helping the Committee come to its own final decision. In truth, no one seriously thought that they could scare up enough money to provide rail transportation for the entire team unless the players themselves could come up with a good portion of the money. That being a proposition as unlikely as getting the Municipality to help, in the end, they turned to those sports-minded citizens of Turnbull and district who owned automobiles. The Committee expected, of course, to pay the cost of gasoline.

A simple proposition on the surface; still, there was a problem in all this. With rare exception, car owners of the period were in the habit of setting their respective vehicles up on blocks the last week of November or thereabouts, depending on the earliness of winter. The autos would be left there drained of summer coolant, which was only water—until some time in March when it wasn't too much trouble to re-fill and empty the machine's radiator if a cold snap threatened. A few of the sporting men did keep their machines operating year round mostly gents owning the lighter, sportier, cars: Ford Model-A coupes,

Nash Runabouts and the like. The heavy machines, ones with the capacity to take on six passengers and luggage, and Smith-Jones' McLaughlin-Buick for example, could pretty much count on being stored sitting up on blocks until April—earlier if the roads and weather turned favourable.

In those days, only a few owned an automobile. An automobile was a prized possession of which the owners, having great pride in them naturally also took care of them. Often as not, they ran them only during the least destructive road and weather conditions-occurring for mostly a six or seven month period each year. Admittedly, insurance was an equally important factor. Few car owners of the day saw any merit in paying out for insurance for a full year when everyone knew that there was really only six months of decent driving conditions anyhow. It was hard to argue the logic of paying out for six months insurance versus twelve.

"If we persuade say Smith-Jones to lend his car, what about insurance?" Carl Gassing put in.

The Mayor, being an insurance agent himself, responded, "Gentleman I'm glad Carl raised the question for I have a solution. Mutual, company I represent, has a short term insurance policy … has a minimum of one week for just such occasions. Naturally, I'll wave my commission."

"And my shop will check out any machine for anyone who is willing to lend it. No charge there either." Carl spoke up in support.

"Well done!" said my father expressing the view of the entire committee.

This discussion may seem foreign to a modern reader but, as I have said, at the time, most automobiles were put into storage a-waiting spring. These potential arrangements, as far as the Committee was concerned were the clinchers as to whether or not the team would go by automobile. The Mayor also figured on the Team paying half of the small premium, in addition to his offer to waive his own personal fees for writing up the insurance. He topped off the offer by the lending of his Dodge Flat Head Six. Still, a few cynics believed that the

Mayor's largess, never one of his stronger suits, was due to acute embarrassment suffered in the Grandad Cade affair. However, to give credit where credit is due it did give a kick-start in the right direction.

Looking back now, I am less quick to judge the reluctance of the automobile owners of the day remembering that it did take considerable time and preparation to take the family auto off the blocks and then make sure it was road worthy as well.

The first task, always, was lowering of the vehicle wheel by wheel until it was firmly resting upon the ground. Followed then by reversing the wintering process and refilling the radiator with fresh water before starting it up to see if would still run. Of course, after first checking the oil and protecting the motor from possible overnight freezing as well as re-inflating the tube type natural rubber tyres—the blocking up was done for the sake of the tyres; the thinking being that contact with the earth would cause them to deteriorate more quickly. In addition, the air pressure was dropped to reduce sidewall cord strain, steel and polyester not then in use. So these considerations, as well as the matter of insurance played a part in the owner's decision to let out his auto or not. Moreover, once having gotten the machine ready there was still the bother of draining and re-filling the radiator or finding some heated garage space again in order to prevent a burst radiator. Carl Gassing, forever ready to go the extra mile, offered, on a first come basis, to make overnight room at his service garage for anyone willing to volunteer their automobile and at no charge. Overall, my father reported, the meeting had gone well.

"Nothing like a big game to get the locals pulling together for a change," he pronounced, pleased with the proceedings.

Next day, around four-thirty, the Mayor with a couple of henchmen and team officials and coach—Turk McKenzie and money manager Doc Rafferty—arrived at the rink whilst I was getting some instructions from the Captain. Turk McKenzie, looking discomforted at being part of the entourage, mumbled a nearly inaudible hello—the Mayor looking official and Doc Rafferty maintaining a practised formality befitting the occasion.

"Christ!" the Captain swears under his breath and startling me since he was not prone to swear except on rare occasions. Admittedly, he sometimes muttered a mild oath in reference to the Mayor and Council. Moreover, he had a well-established practise of handing out 'Ice-time holidays' for any kid caught swearing in a public place.

"You want to swear?" he would challenge, "Then do it at the pool hall."

This admonishment was always greeted in silence since the violators were not old enough to be there in any case. So for him to swear aloud was quite startling. It was followed by an under the breath apology while trying to muster some degree of politeness for the delegation. He did so by busying himself at an inconsequential task before stopping to fill his pipe and feigning a sudden awareness of their presence.

"Ah good afternoon Mr. Simpson," said the Mayor in a manner certain to infuriate the Captain. Captain Jack paused taking time to clean out his pipe with a penknife before he spoke, stalling I expect and forcing the Mayor to continue on talking. "See you are busy as always," said the Mayor rather solicitously, and while not exactly afraid of the Captain's well known quick tongue, he did not want to provoke the Captain into any sort of sidetracking issue.

By the tone of voice, you knew he had come asking for something out of the ordinary and knowing my Father headed the Hockey committee; he made some unctuous remark about my being that fine Sinclair boy. I thought he was about to pat me on the head as he said it but he didn't.

Captain Jack eventually stopped the pipe fiddling and, to my surprise, courteously acknowledged each member of the group many of whom he actually liked. There was, I thought, no accounting for the ways of adults, not having yet learned that courtesy even to one's political enemies was a necessity in a small community where one could come face-to-face with either friend or foe literally on a daily basis. It was a learned skill enabling one to negotiate through life's daily trials. I think, in Captain Jack's case, he was the epitome of the archetypal grumbling Canadian worker neither thinking of himself as a boss nor a manager although those are exactly the roles the Captain assumed each year he ran the rink. That being said I suspected that if Captain Jack actually had to arrange the financing and address himself to the political realities of serving and satisfying various pressure groups, he would have sounded a retreat rather quickly. Moreover, while he felt free to criticize, he liked the job and, I was learning, knew quite well, who was paying him to do so. Still, as quickly as he could acknowledge this failing in his character, he was prone to launch a new attack upon all those things he felt were wrong-headed or misguided by those who governed. His excuse for not taking up these challenges was that he had insufficient education to do the job. Be that as it may, being around Captain Jack was an education in itself because of his virtues and even some of his inadequacies. Like most, I have my own acquired idiosyncrasies staying on with me for a lifetime.

Much to the Captain's surprise, the thing that brought the Mayor and his entourage to the rink was nothing more than a desire to see first hand if money might be needed for rink or equipment repairs. "Big time," the Captain kept repeating happily after they had taken their leave. But before that happened the Captain, nearly dumbstruck, took them on a tour pointing out every boarded over window and needed stove pipe replacement adding in a few board feet of lumber but, strangely, made no mention of the pump belt.

"Didn't want them to think I couldn't see to things. Besides it'll hold now till next year though if they had brought me a new one I wouldn't have wasted so much time," was his excuse and final say in the matter, he pronounced, when in all innocence, I had asked him why he was willing to wait. Needless to say, nothing essential was missed and both he and the delegation seemed satisfied when it was over.

5

This aging of body is not supposed to happen to boyhood heroes like Turk McKenzie. Heroes are to stay the same, which is why they are best kept in the recesses of the mind, fresh, young, invincible. Physically, he resembled former hockey great Lanny McDonald. Not surprising when one considers the common heritage, not to mention the moustache, which was common in that day—red of course. If one believed in re-incarnation perhaps this would be a case to ponder. Yet, I do not actually know if Turk was a star in his own day. I heard enough mentioned to know that he had been good, possibly better than just good. He was youthful and vibrant although given to few words. My cousin Busher allowed that Turk didn't need to do a lot of talking you just knew when he was satisfied and when he was not. Of course, there were set practise routines, which he established at the beginning of each season and, as far as I know, he was never much for varying them. Warm ups, some skill demonstrations, a little talk on strategies then lots of practise of one on twos, one on ones, alone in on the goalie, followed by a short scrub game and final skates around the ice before going off. These routines were very similar to those given us by our Pee Wee level coach but with less of the technical stuff. He had us concentrate more upon learning how to be a good skater. I remember, I hated having to skate backwards with out a hockey stick in hand as a kind of life support and steering mechanism. I was certain, that without it, I would fall on my head and take a terrible fall.

Still, like the rest, I learned and eventually stopped trying to see behind and developed enough confidence to know where both ice and feet were in relation to one and other. It's a bit like a swimming backstroke. It takes practise before you are confident that you will stop your back motion before, not after, hitting the pool edge. Nor did I like skating clockwise, although Captain Jack, on the side of coaches, declared that some part of an evening or afternoon skate had to be in that direction. He always claimed it was to keep the ice in shape but in reality, he was trying to foster better skating habits for aspiring hockey players. We believed him because he was protective of his ice surface particularly prior to a Tiger's game. Once, I even got suspended for one day. I foolishly got caught attempting to cut-the-ice—a practise sometimes indulged in by older players showing off their prowess. I knew that Captain Jack had to impose the penalty, so I was simply happy that it was only going to be a short banishment. I doubt that he had the actual authority to serve up these penalties, but no one in the community ever seemed to object. He simply operated the facility much like a baseball Czar. I think his set of rules just crept into the operation and no kid ever thought to challenge him on them. It was as if an ordinance had been written and approved by council just for Captain Jack albeit none seem to exist in the municipal archival records. So many of his successors benefited from his innovative management style, I think it ought to have been given a name. Not exactly *The Peter Principle*, something more uplifting I should like to think.

Sometime back, while at University, Captain Jack's order of things came to mind. It was more a diversion from the technical problems I had been struggling with at Engineering School.

My Liberal Arts friends decline to acknowledge that I was being educated there. Trained, my lawyer friend Vince—whose first degree was of that ilk—was fond of saying, "Not un-useful but still only trained." He does not respond when I tell him I once won a campus essay contest. However, it is a trifling matter and I think I have more time to read the occasional novel or go to theatre than he does in his more corporate world. Nor will I ever confess to having taken an English Lit course albeit after graduation. But enough! My career choice may have been fostered, in part, by my days of hanging around the skating rink and Rafferty's shop. Even idling about at Gassing's had its influence. There, all I wanted was just a word or two from Whizzer Jackson but the hanging out and watching the mechanics work, gave me some insights that proved useful later on in life.

The reason, as I have said, for my lone suspension had to do with trying to cut-the-ice on a single turn. The technique being to force the heel of the blade into the ice in such a way as to scatter a shower of chips up over the rink boards, thus putting on an imagined great display of skill and muscle; "yahoos" declared Captain Jack. While I did not wish to be regarded as a 'Yahoo' in his books, at the same time I did not want to be known as someone too unskilled or too prissy to have never tried.

My timing was bad. Captain Jack, but an hour before, banned a Juvenile player for the night—it seemed the holidays he handed out, for minor offences, were a little less stern as you got older. Yet, showing off did sometimes cause ice damage to the extent that the Captain had to go out during a free skate evening and make repairs. His fear simply being that some patron might unknowingly catch a skate blade in the ruts and possibly sustain a bad fall. And, this is just what happened to my cousin Janet Blair. She had to have stitches placed in her leg, after catching a skate blade in just such a cut; she crashed into the sideboards. Foolishly, that evening I took on a dare not knowing the Captain had just made some repairs at the other end of the rink. Paddy had set me up and I didn't know it. I was, at the time, inside the rink shack and thinking that the Captain was probably also inside at the very same moment telling one of his many stories while warming himself in front of the Quebec heater. It was something he often did just before blinking the rink lights to indicate closing time, so I did not bother to check upon his whereabouts.

I, for the first time, succeeded in cutting the turn and if I do say so, managed to scatter a fair bit of ice in the direction of the boards. Although, when I related this feat to a group of sympathetic contemporaries wanting the details of my banishment I was unjustly accused of having most likely cut into a soft and recently repaired ice patch. The injustice of these remarks coupled with the banishment put me in a state of high dudgeon as I wended my way home. In short, my moment of triumph had been snowed on. I was cut to the quick. Worse, I was mortified at having done such a foolish thing thereby forcing the Captain into giving me a two-day Holiday; something he did not really want to do. Still, despite feeling failed and foolish, there was a bit of an up side to it. Grounding me maintained the Captain's reputation for fair play and took away any suggestion, from my contemporaries that I had some kind of a favoured son status, even if, it may have been true. Still, I did not question the fairness of his decision even to myself.

Fern saw me coming home early and naturally wanted to know what was up.

She listened patiently as I recited the gist of what had happened complete with a litany of complaints about my contemporaries; her only comment being, "Well you didn't do anything real bad so I guess it won't affect your job. How deep did you cut the ice anyhow?"

"Well," I began finally getting a sympathetic ear so I told her the full story.

"Gee, I didn't think you could do it," she said, with some admiration, cementing our friendship even more.

Once I was allowed back, nothing further was ever mentioned about it.

An attribute of Captain Jack was his understanding of youth and young boys in particular. It was not exactly what he said or did; it was his way of encouraging and setting of examples with just the right amount of irreverence for officialdom that set him apart, in our eyes, from the majority of the adult world. Whenever we played hockey, he always had an encouraging word as we left the ice regardless of whether we had played brilliantly or poorly, it was always the same.

"Good try lads," he would say whenever we lost the period or the game.

That, and rarely saying much more, as he went about the business of directing his crew of ice cleaners and sweepers before, he himself checked the goal post mounting pins; resetting them if the action had been too brisk and always sprinkling the crease area with hot water—even if the entire sheet did not get a quick re-flooding. Sometimes, for important games, such as the up coming Royals vs. Tigers match, he would have barrels of hot water ready for the second period intermission. This light flooding between periods was accomplished without the aid of machines of any description. Occasionally, his fastidiousness might lead to a slight delay of game. However, his crew of young men who scrapped the ice and then pulled the spray-barrels of water generally managed to get the job done right on time.

During regular games, he simply wandered the ice with a spray can and patched up where ever he found some ice damage. "Look at that," he would say, "… always some young pup showing off to the girls. If I were a girl I wouldn't give his kind the time of day," he would say when he thought some show-off was responsible.

"No sir." I would agree, as I tagged along after the Captain Jack while carrying his scoop shovel.

And, always he would be swearing and grumbling if he thought the damage had been caused by just such a stunt. Thankfully, he was kind enough to never refer to the fact that it was a stunt of the same sort that I had, on that one occasion, tried my hand at, or more properly my feet. During games of lesser importance, his angular face would take on a look of mild disgust before voicing his displeasure aloud to anyone at hand. Then, he would simply walk on leaving the gouges just as they were.

"Those cocky young Studs want to cut up the ice they can just play on it, and if they happen to fall on their backsides, it might give cause to remind them of which part of their thinking anatomy they should be using."

His voice would rise the more he thought of 'Cocky young Studs' wrecking his ice, before realizing that his emotions were showing far more than he cared to have them do; whereupon, he would promptly change the subject to some less fractious topic. I think his lifelong desire to do things rationally was what irked him most about show-off youth. He had himself come from a pioneering existence and showing off, except in the spirit of fun and entertainment, didn't count. Yet he was not a sombre person and liked to tell as well as listen to good clean funny stories, particularly those to do with genuine athletic prowess. Indeed, he had made his own mark playing Snooker, a game in which, he was a superb player and had considerable standing locally; remaining pretty much undefeated until he was quite old. His reputation was further enhanced by once having taken on a touring artist in a series of exhibition games and administering the circuit player a close but decisive defeat. It was said that the loss caused the player to take up the lesser game of pool—so the story goes. As always, he was a gentleman after each game, win or lose, no excuses offered for a loss and some genuine encouragement given to the loser if he won. I had no personal experience in this because; I was not of the age of admission to the local billiard hall during his reign.

Quite the contrary was the Mayor, who liked his accomplishments well lime-lighted. He had been a local athlete of some note and so his offices were lined with team photos, news clippings and the like. Captain Jack never acknowledged the Mayor's prowess by speaking of it but once, I remember Turk McKenzie talking of some spectacular hit on the baseball field that the mayor had made, and the Captain, to my surprise, not only agreed but provided some exacting details about it. This was a bit of a revelation to me, for I knew nothing of yesterday's sports idols and had, yet, to learn how fleeting the limelight sometimes is for many. Nor was I aware of the truism about sports heroes, modern or ancient, having feet of clay.

6

It was official; the Edmonton Royals were coming the second week of February. Archie Macdonald confirmed it. I had gone to see Archie first thing after breakfast. Archie let me ride the dray as he made his rounds—weekends and school holidays—even though it was sometimes slow on Saturday mornings because the CN didn't run a Mail train into Turnbull on that day. On such days, Archie sometimes assisted with our Pee Wee team games, also usually held on Saturdays with the exception of not playing on those days the Tigers had home games. Mostly, we played after school games because the local businessmen profited from big Saturday farm crowd turnouts.

This particular Saturday was not one of those game days for either the Tigers or ourselves nor did Archie have much in the way of deliveries; just one load of coal to the widow Burns, so I decided I might as well go share the news with my buddies.

My mission, of delivering this important news, was cut short; for down the street and walking ahead, was Grandma and my cousin Lisa. I had not seen Lisa since last summer and seeing her now put an ache into my very bones. I hastily stuffed the gum into a pocket and hurried to catch up, quite in contrast to my first meeting with Cousin Lisa last summer, when it had been a duty call; then, I trudged rather than ran. It was not that I did not think well of my relatives, assorted cousins, uncles, aunts on the Stirling side. They were, in the main, nice people, vigorous, honest, and sometimes downright charming. Except Uncle Edgar, him I did not like. Despite, like mother, his having a physical attractiveness as well as a certain outward style, he had an unfathomable unreasonable streak in his makeup that can only be described as egocentric and mean spirited. Lisa had all the Stirling charm with a beauty somehow outside the clan members' basic good looks. Indeed, for a very long time, I pretty much had myself convinced that she must be adopted.

So enamoured was I, the more I contrived to believe that she was not of our blood. That thought adding to my imagination. However, these were feelings rising within me before Mother had sent me off "… to entertain my cousin." Grudgingly, I set off to do her bidding.

"Now James it's not like I was sending you to baby sit or anything like that. Lisa is a fine girl you'll like her."

"Okay Mother," I said giving in and adding, "I'm going.…"

This time, I was quite breathless in my haste to catch up greet her. Her visit was to be short, she said, telling me it was just to visit with Grandma. Grandma had taken a fall and was now recovered from a cracked rib.

This in contrast to last summer when Mother, always looking out for family, wanted me to give Lisa some young person's company, as she put it, which is why I was nominated to be that company and, short of an accident, there was little I could do about it. So my daily fate for a few short weeks was to go to my Grandma's house and hang out with the cousin, show her around and in general try to be a good companion. I soon found myself hardly able to get my chores done before escaping the house. Mother, pleased to see me in the spirit of things expressed her personal gratitude with just a hint of a knowing smile, which I did not catch at the time. I knew later on that she was fully aware of Lisa's charms when first sending me over. Indeed, who would not have been? I mean this in the purest sense. Yet my own feelings, at the time, were too intensely personal to express or share with anybody. Blair, with whom I might have talked, was out of town for that period of time and I guess I never even said much to Fern Appleby although she undoubtedly guessed how I felt. It is still astonishing to me, how most of us can go around thinking that our emotions do not show. Perhaps it is because when we feel passionate about something or someone we oftimes go to great lengths to disguise the fact and succeed in fooling only ourselves.

Our relationship started with me showing her all the local sights I could think of; places an out-of-towner would not likely pick up on. I did avoid the pool hall, where several times, as of a warm spring day, I had witnessed some whistling and the like when a particularly susceptible and pretty young woman chanced by. These little scenes offended my sense of male chivalry, yet I expect, at least some of the young women were flattered by it all. I also, must admit that the pool hall idlers were not the least interested in thirteen year olds even pretty ones like Lisa, but my twelve, going-on-thirteen year old mind was not willing to take any such chance. We spent our happiest, most idle moments at a little fenced off pasture at the edge of town. Someone had dubbed it Shultz Hill even though I never knew of any one named Shultz having lived there nor why it was considered a hill.

Memories of that summer came running through my mind, even when both Grandma and Lisa were greeting me warmly. I tried to sound nonchalant; pleased and offhand, I think was the posture I attempted to put forward and although I do not know what exactly I did say; babbling on, is an appropriate descriptive phrase. Lisa was not quite, as I remembered her. She was still her warm, friendly self, glad to see me and all but…. It was a big but. She had grown several inches taller as well as in all those marvellous ways that young girls do as physically they approach womanhood. She was, only turned fourteen, full of emotion and unsure about the ways of the world yet different. As for me, as I recall, I was at the stage where, while there was a definite push toward young adulthood, I was yet just a boy physically and emotionally hardly a match for a maturing fourteen year old—a fact, which I could not at first, sort out for myself. Grandma brought this difference home to me by insisting that, while she was inviting me for lunch, I must first run home and advise my mother.

The short visit, I soon found out, was only for the weekend. She would return on the next through train. I reported all that I had learned about the upcoming game between The Edmonton Royals and the Turnbull Tigers. Lisa smiled all the while and at the end said it sounded exciting and hoped the local team won. I ran out of meaningful things to say at this point, which was a puzzling experience, because during the summer past our conversations had been endless, our silences bliss. Then, I had been that delectable commodity a nonthreatening yet assessable young male and good looking at that. I checked some old photographs before writing this and I think I am safe in this assertion—the fact that now I am bearded, wear glasses, and have a nose lengthened by living, is beside the point. I was distantly enough related to her for Lisa to feel romantic about and sufficiently close to feel safe about. This was a mutual feeling; the two sides of the same coin if you will. That was yesterday, and much of those feelings were still intact but the romance of it was gone.

Struggling to puzzle out and accept what was the new relationship, I suggested that we might walk over to Shultz Hill even though snow still covered the ground. It brought a momentary smile to her face; even wistful—I do not think I just imagined this part-but also a side-stepping.

"Grandma and I are going to do some things. Please do stay and join us if you would like," was her response.

"No I promised some of the guys I would play street hockey," was my face-saving reply.

I did my best to make it sound like an important commitment knowing full well the informality of street games and that no one playing might even notice my absence. On the way home, I detoured past Shultz Hill trying to re-live some of the past summer now that Lisa's appearance had re-awakened it.

Actually, Shultz Hill was hardly a hill at all it was a tiny knoll. Probably, it was not even a particularly pretty one. Yet it did have charm because it was secluded from the village by a thicket of small willows tucked into a little glen next to one lone but massive balm poplar tree that was set in the midst of a grassy slope and kept groomed by two peaceful dairy cows that grazed there. Nowadays, the same site might well appear as rather untidy—just a bit of rough pasture with a few organic reminders of cows and patches of un-cropped grass. In perspective, those days few homeowners in Turnbull maintained such a thing as a lawn. Even the village athletic park was mostly just a pasture of native grasses that was mowed once or twice each season. One of the mowings usually timed to be done just before Dominion Day on July 1. Other than special times, private yards and village property alike generally received a spring or fall burning off of old grass and weeds, and a once or twice scything around gates and sheds; the playing fields also were given a once over with a horse drawn mower. The local schoolyard was afforded the same spring and fall treatment. The school clean-up being the simplest of the annual clean-ups because a hundred busy young feet kept the major grassed areas worn down. Shultz hill was the nearest thing, at that time, to an actual park. To complete the picture, it had a small pond populated by one muskrat and an occasional duck. For a point of interest, across the north fence stood a haystack-sized pile of fieldstone, which presumably Shultz and his kin had cleared from the pasture. I liked the rock pile for two reasons, one being that a weasel seemed to live within it and secondly, I found it fascinating to watching Blackbirds and Cowbirds scavenge the pile in search of insects and grubs, which they were adept at unearthing from the nooks and crannies.

It was a perfect place when you were twelve and in love. Still it is unlikely that what we had to say to each other was either profound or worth recording. Certainly, I remember little except for what emotional aspects there are that linger on. Sometimes, when some wisp of fragrant spring airlifts my spirits or I see a few beasts grazing about in a similar setting, I am transformed back in time. Then, I remember, Lisa was the first girl, Fern notwithstanding, that I poured out my thoughts and ambitions to. And talk I did. Lisa, bless her innocent young heart did listen. She was so alive and warm—I realize I repeat myself; but only because she is no longer of this earth and I need once again to feel the moment. You see, it was safe for me to pour out my secret desires to Lisa. None of these involved the ambitions of my contemporaries who collectively believed they would become a fireman, farmer, doctor, lawyer, teacher, carpenter or simply a money-maker, and certainly not a writer. None of that for me! I wished, in my most secret being, to become an architect. Before now, I had skirted around the truth even when asked point blank by Fern as to what my ambitions were.

"Jamie you could be almost anything you wanted to be," she countered my evasiveness with a solemnity that startled me. For, at the time, I was not at all certain of my abilities.

Alas, what I told Lisa never came about. I did not become an architect. Close though, as a structural engineer I have worked with many. And, I am content with my lot, long ago realizing I lacked the necessary artistic vision to be truly successful in that profession.

Then, the dream of youth was hazy. Yet, I had read of Christopher Wren. His name came up so often in the historically based adventure I loved to read which is why I set about finding more about him and his achievements. First the encyclopaedia at school, and then a few upper grade histories found in our school's modest library. Also, I had seen one or two reproductions of Leonardo De Vinci's drawings and sketches giving me some insight into Doc Rafferty's fascinating sketches of things he had contemplated building. Moreover, I had opinions. I hated buildings adorned with gingerbread facades and was struck by the functionality of Roman and Greek styles. My architectural experience, of course, was taken all from books. Looking back, I wonder at the incongruity of a love-struck twelve-year musing over pictures of ancient ruins trying to impress a blossoming young woman more interested in shades of lipstick. I hasten to add that this does not indicate shallowness on her part. Lisa was never shallow and to imply that I merely wished to impress is also wrong; there were those elements, of course. Adolescent uncertainties about life aside, our relationship was embraced by a genuine fondness for each other; we related, shared one and the others dreams, aspirations, and delighted in mutual conversational ramblings. Somehow, that closeness had faded and now I was clearly no more than the well liked but much younger cousin. My summer memories, then in essence, part of the journey of growing up. It was, however, too short a time to love, and have lost. On Sunday, she left for home, unromantically taking the supper hour through-train, which could be flagged and slowed down enough for an agile passenger to jump aboard and be off.

That about describes it all, and, as I stood watching the train disappear, I willed my being back into time to that other Saturday of her leaving.

On that day, my mother and Aunt Polly, who had come to visit Grandma, had persuaded Uncle Hart, who lived over at Kings Town, to spend the day and drive us all the fifteen miles to Princess Beach for a picnic and a swim. He agreed, it being Saturday and knowing neither Polly's husband nor my father was able to go. Of course, as he liked them both, it gave him his opportunity to visit with both Lisa and Aunt Polly who were leaving on the Sunday.

As I recall, we all wore those dreadful woollen bathing suits. The itch and smell of wet wool still tingles my skin and nose at the least provocation. I need not explain the itch to those who have worn such garments nor the odour that came from the off seasonal storage in mothballs—a prudent if enduringly odorous method of preventing the garment from being decorated with holes. I had few opportunities to wear my own bathing suit, largely because there was no family vehicle to take us to the beach; consequently, it had become a bit more moth eaten than most. Alas, it had also gotten progressively less stylish with the passage of time. Lisa wore a one-piece, belted suit with red and white trim, which I thought to be just the height of fashion. Aunt Polly had thought to buy it new. In it, Lisa just knocked the eyes out.

In contrast, mine was a one piece tank top suit all one colour, blue as I remember it, with dark red trim around the arm and leg holes. At first, I was embarrassed wearing it because there was yet another moth hole which mother had somehow overlooked and forgotten to mend. Lisa full of kindness and ignoring the mends said it looked good on me.

"Think so?" I responded pleased and somewhat relieved because she did not appear to have noticed the small hole. Even so, I attempted to hide it while out of the water by turning slightly sideways even when it was not appropriate to do so.

Uncle thought the whole matter of the hole to be quite amusing yet, realizing my discomfort, did his best to reassure me. He made light of the matter, as we did our changing on our allotted side of the car. There being no dressing houses, our choice was to either dress in the nearby bushes or, as Uncle did on this occasion, drive his car just beyond the tree line; our beach side dressing rooms created by draping a car blanket over one set of windows and deciding, then, which side was ladies and which side men's. Uncle declared the driver's side to be ours. When uncle thought that sufficient time had passed for the ladies to change, he simply hollered out that he and I were ready and heading to the beach. The ladies thus warned, we angled ourselves away from the automobile, gentlemanly declining to look back.

During the proceedings, while Uncle and I said little, we could hear mother and Aunt Polly chortling noisily like a couple of young schoolgirls. I remember thinking that they ought to have been more dignified since they were mothers and all—so much for my generational perspective. As for me, all formality was forgotten immediately Lisa took my hand and together we dashed through the shallows flopping onto the incoming waves and leaving aunt and mother standing sedately on shore, while uncle taking his own pleasure moved to deeper water for a swim. Uncle, who was balding and unromantic to look at, had, at the same time, a fair good command of the water. He was the 'wet your-ankles and plunge' type. He did just that and was soon frog kicking beyond our depth. Because neither Lisa nor I had learned much about swimming, we both did a kind of dog paddle and were content to splash around shallower water; sometimes diving and dumping one and other and in between times retreating to shore to work on a sand castle whenever we had enough of the cool water. Lisa fully clothed was one thing, in a clinging wet bathing suit quite another. While the woollen material covered the body, at the same time the clinging nature of it revealed every bit of girlish softness and roundedness underneath. Something, I think, not always intended by the wearers of those dark coloured suits of the day.

Gentlemen, of course, pretended that there was nothing to see. My adolescent being was not that conditioned and so I was all too conscious of anatomical differences. There were times on that afternoon, I confess, when I found it prudent to stay waist deep in the water. Other times when dawdling in the water seemed out of keeping I would do a great lot of splashing then run in out of the water at high speed and fling myself face down upon the sand. Curiously, my thoughts were pristine. Sex and love somehow divorced, such were my notions of male female relationships at the time. Still I did want to kiss her even if just once but never having kissed a girl in seriousness I did not know how to go about it.

Going home, we pressed close together, our knees up on the back seat, together peering out the rear window pretending intense interest in the darkening night sky. Aunt Polly, also sitting in back, sat in the other corner and occupied herself in a running conversation with mother and uncle riding up front. We were physically closer during that half hour ride than we had ever been before. For a time we surreptitiously held hands and because it was dark by the time we arrived home, I almost gathered the courage to ask if I could kiss her, not knowing in my innocence, that a kiss is a spontaneous thing unspoken and mutual. So, intense and wishing, I looked dumbly into her eyes like some hapless puppy and held hands.

Next day, Saturday, was to be the last day of the summer visit and already I was fearful that somehow we would have little chance to spend any of it together and alone. Uncle dropped mother and me off first. I could think of nothing to say that might confirm a meeting next day. I got out of the car with mother mute and devoid of speech. Lisa spoke a halfhearted good-bye that I was afraid might mean just that. I did know that the family would all see them off on the train next day but that was too public for saying farewells. Uncle's shiny black Model-A bounced away leaving me standing on the road. Lisa looked wistfully out the back window. Aunt Polly climbed into the front with Uncle and didn't seem to notice. Mother had already entered the house

Because we had bathed at the beach, I was able to forgo the Saturday night tub scrub. After a late supper, I moped around for a while, stood on the back porch doing nothing and pretended to read comics in the front room.

Mother solved matters. "Dear would you mind running an errand over to Grandma's. I have a note for Aunt Polly. I know you must be tired but if you wouldn't mind?"

Mother was on to me but I was feeling too melancholy and anxious to realize she knew how enamoured I was—I refuse, to this day, to demean the feelings by referring to it as puppy love; a term of the day applied to anyone particularly very young and not of marriageable age. This careless equating of emotions, was, I suppose, about on the same level as melting ice cream. I submit that it was, and is, more profound than that.

I do not remember specifically what the errand was about; I customarily respected the privacy of a folded note unless the sender alerted me as to its contents. Something to do with after Church I think; at any rate, I delivered it unread. Aunty studied the note, smiled, made a few agreeable sounds and maintained, I thought, a curiously expressionless countenance. I did not see Lisa about and was afraid that she had gone to bed or something of the sort for it was actually only eight-thirty; still I was uncertain and a lot of silly things ran through my head.

"Sit down Jamie. I imagine you will want to visit with Lisa for a time. She will be right down. She is upstairs helping your grandmother with some tidying."

Grandma's house—my Grandfather had died when I was quite young so I never really knew him—was of a once familiar pattern. An upstairs with two tiny bedrooms tucked under the eaves and a bit of attic storage space—you can still find some remnants of the style in small prairie towns. It was, I think of the type shipped out across the country by Eaton's. They were solidly built, serviceable houses pre-packaged with all components ready for assembly and quite a bit more than today's stick-built packages but a little less than a modern day factory assembled one. Oftimes one sees them going down the road on a flat bed heading for a country or suburban housing development. Back then, of course, the flatbed was a freight train rail car and the house owner arranged his own delivery from train station to final destination.

Lisa and I went for a last walk. She had braided her hair into pig-tails, making her look younger, more adventuresome and, in my eyes, even prettier than ever. I remember she had on her most favourite hand knit sweater—one I liked best—and wore a pair of pale blue cotton slacks. My description seems unromantic, I realize, awkward even, but she had an appealing openness about her, a characteristic I remember to this day and these mundane details serve to evoke that which I feel. Even her choice of dress put me at ease, somehow eliciting feelings of confidence and protectiveness. The walk was ritual. We toured the town. Walked by, but not down to Schultz Hill for it was, as I have said, already nighttime. I was taken by her every gesture, as well as every word and bit of silliness that passed between us. I remember, vividly, the thrill of thinking her being thirteen ... thirteen and had never, not even once, alluded to the fact that I was younger.

Eventually—too soon—our walk came to an end. The time for a formal goodbye had come. We stood in darkness by Grandma's front gate sheltered by an enormous lilac bush, out of sight and away from lights.

There is, I have learned over time, little to say at any age on such occasions. We talked a bit of trivia and promised faithfully to write to one and other. We tried "goodbye"; one would say it, a touching of hands, a turn to go, and then, "I forgot to tell you ..." It went on like this for a time until we both realized that it was getting late and we would have some explaining to do if we did not soon arrive home. Mother would be worrying. Aunty would be worrying.

At last, "I've got to go now Jamie." Sensible Lisa took the initiative. I tugged at her hands. "Close your eyes Jamie." I did as told scarcely breathing, my heart pounding. "I'll miss you Jamie," she said softly and as she spoke, I felt her warm lips press fleetingly upon my own. She drew back and started away. "Stay where you are until you see my light." I nodded dumbly a thousand frogs welling up in my throat preventing me from speaking.

I do not know exactly how long it was I waited, not long, I think, although the passage of time escaped my consciousness, obscuring reality. It was long enough however for me to begin feeling a little uncomfortable and I tried to think of some plausible reason for standing there in the dark should someone I knew happen upon me.

Lisa's room light came on, and then went off. I watched as the curtains drew open. I imagined but could not actually see her form there in the dark and my heart once again began to pound. The light came back on. Lisa, warm lovely Lisa, stood naked at the casement, briefly but forever. Too soon, the curtains were drawn, the lights turned out. I walked home in silence unable to adequately express my thoughts even to myself. I barely made my presence known to my mother and father and headed straight to bed where I lay awake for what seemed like hours. When I awoke in the morning, it was with a sense of wonder and loss.

I remember now, not exact details, only impressions and charged emotions of that night. I can still visualize taking leave of Lisa; still picture, although I have none of her at that age, her great charm, her loveliness. It is possible she is prettier in my memory than she was in life. She is forever the girl of last summer.

But on this, the last summer, I was simply the nice younger cousin waiting my time to metamorphose.

I found the shinny game. It was being played over on Blair's street. I watched for a while and said I would go home and get my stick, which I did not do. Somehow, it was important to talk to someone. Just to sort out some things in my head. My hockey playing buddies were out of the question. Nor were any of the adults I might have confided in. Captain Jack crossed my mind so did Archie but they were, well, too adult to understand. I crossed the street from my home and called on Fern. She was my buddy when, of course, I was not pursuing the fortunes of the Turnbull Tigers and Whizzer Jackson. Fern, well it's hard to explain exactly but we talked about things I did not choose to talk about even with my closest male friend: secret ambitions (Christopher Wren) why birds could fly as they did and man could not: sex—did girls think about sex as often as boys? In my experience, girls seemed to know more about it than boys. Some, I knew, could be quite clinical about the matter especially during mixed-sex playground gatherings when no one wanted to play field games, tag or the like—the kind of day when it was better to sit in the shade than play out in the sun. Fact, fantasy, gossipy bits and the telling of very juvenile jokes characterized those impromptu sex-education sessions. Jokes that neither bear repeating nor have they left anything of significance in my memory bank. I just know that this puberty interest existed and that I doubt if much of it could be characterized as enlightened. Even at that, the information gathered was probably a cut above those dreadful 'What Every Boy Ought to Know' books, which parents or ministers sometimes handed out and were most always two years too late in context and contained nothing of practical value in any case. However, it was not of those sorts of things of which I wished to talk. Indeed, talk was not even it. I simply had a need to visit with someone with whom talk was possible and silence acceptable. The mysterious age of fourteen and young womanhood was a puzzle needing some unraveling and Fern was the person with whom to begin.

7

"Got a nickel?" I asked Blair.

"Two pennies ..." he dug into his pocket and I followed suit coming up with four.

"We'll make like we are looking for a Captain Marvel." I headed confidently for the door, Blair following now that we had an acceptable ploy for being in the store. Smith-Jones did not allow loitering and would question us upon entry. As expected, we had hardly entered before he turned his eyes away from the delegation.

"Got some money? You might find a few out-of-dates in back but don't touch any tied bundles; there are no comics amongst them," he warned.

"Thank you Mr. Smith-Jones," I said in my most mannerly voice, Blair chiming in as we did our best to look like genuine customers and found our way to the back bookstand where the Distributor's returns were stacked. The arrangement with the suppliers was to tear off the covers of all dated magazines and return them for a partial rebate. Out-dated and cover-less copies would then be sold at a discount. This may sound like a great deal and in a way it was but only if you did not wish to view the glossy covers full of the neat doings of Captain Marvel or Batman and Robin who were our personal favourites. The covers also contained information on joining fan clubs as well as details for ordering secret code rings and the like. I never actually joined or bought a code ring but I thought a lot about it.

Once Smith-Jones seemed to forget about the two of us we took the opportunity to peek into a *Blue Book* magazine, which we found fascinating because of its lurid sketches, usually of some spectacularly built female in the clutches of a scoundrel of one sort or another. I read a few *Blue Book* stories later in life and discovered that they were predictable adventures having clearly defined good guys and bad guys. A kind of latter day western set in exotic places—the rescued lady providing innocent and sometimes mysterious romantic elements that pale by today's standards. However, when you were twelve, it was a glimpse into the unknown. We missed some of the conversation—what we had come in for—because, given this unusual opportunity of not having Smith-Jones hovering about monitoring, we became engrossed in story illustrations, and sketches, which we found irresistible. That was so because we did not know of a real live woman or girl of the proportions depicted by the artists although, Blair and I both agreed that Marsha Fisher came close.

The Mayor was the first to speak, after Judge Whittaker, Doc Rafferty, and Turk McKenzie each in turn proffered a noon time greeting, saying things like: "Afternoon John ... or John, got the store looking very fine," and the like.

"As you can probably guess John we are here for the Hockey Committee, myself and the Judge here, representing the Village of course. Carl Gassing was unable to get away."

"I can see that. What is it today gentlemen. Need a donation or some supplies at cost, I am always glad to oblige."

Smith-Jones, having met with delegations before, got right down to business. Blair looked at me knowingly when he heard supplies mentioned, but that was not what it was about. The Mayor quickly launched into a plea for the McLaughlin-Buick, carefully going over the ground as to how the Municipal Council had as usual denied Turnbull any assistance other than a heartfelt professing of good will and moral support. The others were content to let the Mayor do the talking and merely nodded in assent at each point made. Smith-Jones, business-like as always, cut through the Mayor's verbiage and offered his own opinion about the matters presented.

"Gentlemen, I understand the dilemma and have thought about the matter myself. You wish to put my name and, of course, my

McLaughlin-Buick at the top of your list so you can say even Smith-Jones is willing …"

"Well, I … wouldn't exactly put it quite that way John." The Mayor tried to look a little offended at the suggestion that they might be using the good name of Smith-Jones merely to further their cause. Nevertheless, that was precisely the ploy and all present knew it.

The request had more to it than first meets the eye and I expected Smith-Jones to give the matter considerable thought; because, the practise, back then, was to store one's vehicle over winter, putting the vehicle up on blocks and then leaving it to sit unused until well into the spring of the next year. To change from this routine meant that despite spring, and gophers practically just around the corner, it all added up to at least a half-day's work by a competent service man, if all went well. In addition to all this, each night—few auto owners of those days had heated garages—the water coolant would have to be completely drained from the engine each time the automobile was left overnight. During the day, for just a few hours, a heavy blanket could be draped over the hood of the machine. Smith-Jones, being of conservative mind in matters both personal and business, was not likely, I thought, to carry out these preparations in advance of the proper season. His would be, I reasoned, a carefully calculated review of every aspect of this annual spring auto inspection and readiness; it could be seen as a rather tiresome attitude for a sporting man but probably an admirable attribute for a pharmacist.

"Well gentleman," said Smith-Jones after a long pregnant pause, as they say, a bemused look upon his face and an air about him as if he were dealing children. "I am more flattered than offended." Predictably he made no immediate decision, "Of course I shall have to give the matter some thought before I lend my name and of course my automobile. And you know if conditions do not permit the use of the automobile I most …" his voice trailed off.

"Naïve, even for Whittaker and the Mayor," was my father's response upon learning of the details of their meeting.

At the heart of the matter was the fact that the McLaughlin-Buick in question was no ordinary one even for an auto of that calibre. Now, it was not exactly like the gold plated models beloved by some potentates, but it did have a lot of fancy extra equipment: including a fold out bar, jump seats and, to use a term of modern hucksters—and much, much more! The most important added equipment was the hidden bar. Quite surprising actually, considering that Smith-Jones was Presbyterian by upbringing and United Church by choice. Moreover, the Alberta society of the late thirties still carried much of the trappings of prohibition and held decidedly, if but lingering, Calvinistic attitudes about any form of drink stronger than lemonade or cocoa. Certainly strong drink was neither to be seen nor taken of in a public place! Hence, the hidden back seat foldout bars.

The bar did get used, for it was the custom of Smith-Jones during the summer, and particularly as of a Sunday afternoon ball game, to arrive early at the ball grounds, before the game's start, so that he could park his McLaughlin-Buick in an advantage spot. Typically, he parked it behind the extended backstop that had been erected to protect the home team dugout. There he and his buddies had the pleasure of being the first to learn of bench decisions as well as having a splendid view of the game. The chicken wire strung over the backstop also served to screen parked automobiles from any errant balls hitting a windscreen, albeit it was there primarily to discourage exuberant fans, friendly or hostile, from interfering with players and team managers, particularly during ball tournaments.

Smith-Jones routine was always the same. First, he would bring two canvas lawn chairs from the trunk of the car. These he set out beside his auto always behind the wire screen and at the passenger side, the bar being convenient to that side, also more discreetly kept from the public eye. Carl Gassing, or one of the other inner circle buddies, also parked one or more vehicles behind the wire screen adjacent to the McLaughlin-Buick. It was there, then, that Smith-Jones and his friends maintained a certain private access to his car and the aforementioned foldout bar. The drinks were always poured into tall, leather sheathed highball glasses filled with previously mixed gin cocktails, which he and his cronies consumed during the game.

Mrs. Smith-Jones, said to be of a delicate and gentle nature, never attended these outings. According to the captain, she did not attend because more likely she thought the game to be much too common for her tastes. "Too hoity-toity," he would add. The Captain's assessment aside, the ball games were not too common for Smith-Jones himself though he tended to call out a few Cricket match terms during the excitement of a particularly fine play. These gaffs were likely brought on by more than one re-fill into his leather-encased glass. I suppose one should not have been surprised by it, since Smith-Jones, having had no sons who might have played, had little reason to become particularly well versed in the North American game. Certainly, going for gin and cucumber sandwiches rather than beer and popcorn did not quite make it in our town. To be honest, I never actually saw cucumber sandwiches. I refer to them only to make a point.

Canadian mores seemingly just escaped Smith-Jones' attention or he found them too colonial for his tastes. What puzzled my contemporaries and me was that despite his old country ways, he had a good grasp of our beloved hockey game. Possibly, the game being foreign to him and so 'Canadian' he felt compelled to make a study of its intricacies. Also—a picky point—one did not bring gin cocktails into the ice-rink, particularly not in leather covered drink containers and go un-noticed, not even Smith-Jones could get away with that. Tongues would be clacking and Mrs. Smith-Jones would know about it even before he got home. All that aside, he rarely attended games other than those of the Tigers and yet, as I have said, he seemed well versed about hockey in general. Other times, non-skater that he was, he did not come near the rink. Even now, it does not surprise me to think that he may have thought it as his civic duty to be better versed about hockey. Then again, he did have some sporting blood in him, as they used to say.

Smith-Jones suddenly appeared above us as we were sprawled on the floor enjoying our illicit browsing. Smith-Jones, it seemed, had four eyes in his head so good was he at picking out the activities of wayward boys such as us.

"Well now John you think about what we said. The town and the team is going to be counting on you," called out the Mayor putting the best light on the matter as the delegation having gotten as far as it could in their quest were then exiting the store. Their departure also temporarily distracted Smith-Jones from dealing with us.

"As I said, we shall just have to see how things evolve. Everything in its own time and place," was Smith-Jones' parting response and for him a "we'll see," meant not at all. "I shall try my best," meant only if there was no way out; and even an actual commitment was tempered with a provision concerning "no unforeseen circumstances." Smith-Jones looked for as many unforeseen possibilities right down o the last moment of decision. Even so, a sudden change of voice alerted us to the fact that there were a few things that did get Smith-Jones' immediate attention.

"What,' he demanded, "were we doing?"

Blair, with surprising inventiveness, stated that we were just looking through the discards at the pictures and found some pretty funny pictures in the grown-up magazines as well. His countenance was an unexpected picture of innocence throwing Smith-Jones quite off guard and saving me, usually the spokesmen, from making some idiotic response.

"Well then bring your purchases to the counter if you are buying. Come back another day if you are not. You've had enough time to decide, don't you agree."

"Yes sir," we replied in unison.

Smith-Jones having recovered his usual aplomb and brisk manner escorted Blair and me to the front of his store and we left without spending our combined cache of pennies. However, we had picked up, first hand, some exclusive information, which we were now eager to share. We decided that first off we would tell Captain Jack and then maybe Arch Macdonald and our moms.

But when it got right down to it what really did we have to tell?

Finally, after a week of nervous expectation, the school week was over and the big day was almost upon us. The Edmonton City Royals arrived on the six o'clock passenger train.

An official delegation including the Mayor, Turk McKenzie, along with other notables connected to hockey with the exception of Captain Jack, who we knew would be at the rink readying the Royals equipment room.

Aside from the team officials and coach, the Edmonton team appeared to be better than average in height and weight; giving us cause to wonder if the Turnbull Tigers may have taken on more than they were going to be able to handle. Impressive physical presence was not all of it. Where our guys were, in truth a bit of a motley crew to look at, dressed in whatever suited the individual members, the Royals also looked ever-so-sharp in their snappy, double breasted, Melton cloth overcoats .They were of the kind that had a belt in the back and a fashionable notched collar. If they had been made of cotton, you could have imagined Bogart as their leader. And to top it all, each team member had a colourful Frasier woollen scarf about the neck, although there was no indication that any of the players were actually of Scottish origin. Later, I was to learn that the scarves were a gift of their principal sponsor and that these young men each had purchased the coats independently obviously from the same clothier, who undoubtedly would have given each player a discount. The team also gifted their gloves. Attire aside, most of the young men were bare headed. At the time, I thought it very smart practise. Indeed, more so when I looked about at the greeting party, lead by the Mayor, who wore a tatty old coat which he had owned as long as living memory. Turk McKenzie, part of the delegation looked as solid as ever; yet, I felt slightly embarrassed that he had worn his customary tweed cap and a longish scarf draped over a colourful Mackinaw I had once admired. A coat, I now thought, not suited to the splendour of the occasion. And, although personally I knew little nor even cared much about fashion, the Royals were making a great impression upon me and largely because of their style. I remember rather self-consciously adjusting my leather helmet so that the straps were tied at the top rather than letting the flaps hang open and dangling down past my ears. I suppose I thought to show a little style myself.

Once the initial pleasantries were over, the entire entourage moved on leaving behind the equipment manager to take care of the gear. Blair and I, having been delegated by Captain Jack, got to ride the dray—stacked high with equipment—to the rink. Arch even let us sit atop the pile, giving us further cause to feel important.

The manager and coach, accompanied by an entourage of village dignitaries and team officials, escorted the Royals first to the hotel where a fortunate few were allotted prime rooms. The remaining players were then taken to various billets about town. The Mayor and his entourage then led the Royal officials into the Hotel's reception room, for what Captain Jack described, as a few snorts. Arch, despite the importance of the hockey gear, took his usual about town route, stopping first at the post office where Blair and I were allowed to carry in a couple of the smaller bags, but not being authorized personnel, we had to stop at the door of the sorting room itself. The post office always comes first, Arch told us, because The King's Mail has priority over all express deliveries. Moreover, the locals, already waiting outside the closed wicket, took the matter just as seriously as the Postal Agent himself. Arch however having some official status did carry the mail bags directly into the sorting room where the mail, once sorted, was eventually handed out to the public during official open hours. I always found this little ritual of Arch actually going behind the closed doors quite impressive as, under normal circumstances, no outsider was ever allowed to enter into the mailroom. "The mail ...,"said the Postmaster rather pompously, "... is the business of His Majesty and the Dominion Government."

After the mail, came the delivery of any perishables to the local general and grocery stores then finally the rink delivery. One box of produce, I noticed, was marked "Special and Rush". I knew this would be for the banquet supper.

On this pre-game first night, the two teams would take supper together at the 'Chinaman's'—as Lee Changs's Chinese and Western Cuisine was commonly known. In those days, whenever an important supper or special occasion was forthcoming, it was always held at the Chinaman's. The meal was paid for by the town and was an informal friendly gesture to welcome the occasion of a hockey team of calibre; particularly since not every small town got to host such a team. It was also considered only sporting that the members of the two teams should get to know one another informally. This did not detract, I hasten to add, from the sincere desire of each team to defeat the other nor would it likely lessen the physical aspects of the game; moreover, it was assumed that all play would be done in a very sportsman like manner with the best team winning.

Quite different from modern times; the game officials also attended so that they might field any questions from either side as to how the game was going to be called. Sandy Tompkins was the referee for this occasion—never a better choice. Sandy was fair, decisive, and, the local view was that he would throw his own brother out of the game if it came to that. Of course, by this time neither Sandy nor his brother played any serious hockey. Sandy might have made the semi-pros but had come to our town instead to play hockey and teach school. He had a family and mouths to feed and the decision had not been too difficult to make for Pros in those days only got paid while they played and usually had to find off-season jobs. The difference was that Sandy only had to find an off-season job for two months as a teacher and, fortuitously, Sandy was a terrific short stop and played each summer for the Turnbull Major Baseball team. Sandy taught high school math, which perhaps accounted for his brisk no nonsense manner on and off the playing field.

It only took about fifteen minutes to deliver the mail and the perishables before we were on our way to the rink.

We unloaded at the Ladies, skate room, I was a little awed by it because boys were not allowed to enter and so this was my first time there. I do not now know what it was I expected but I remember being surprised that it wasn't any different than the Men's skate room except of course there was no graffiti on the walls and it some how looked better preserved. It had a Quebec heater central and near the wall to the right as you came in. On the left and at the back sat built in benches and two short moveable ones. In the corner furthest from the stove was a shelf holding a bucket of water. A galvanized dipper hung from a nearby nail—just like in the Men's.

I really thought that somehow, the Ladies' would have had a bit of female graffiti scrawled upon the walls. What exactly, I did not know but its lack puzzled me. While Captain Jack discouraged it in the Men's he never removed it either. Mind he would not stand for any foul language; that could also get you a Weeks Holiday. Most of the stuff was comic strip in character with words enclosed in cartoon style balloons. I think one reason Captain Jack never removed anything is because some forgotten wag had depicted the Mayor with whip in hand and a Simon Legree character named the Captain on the receiving end. I think he secretly revelled in it and, because it was not prominently displayed—he could choose to ignore it.

There was also one and one only Team dressing room. The room, for ordinary games, was oftimes given over to the visiting team and that applied all the way up to Midgets. At the time, the designation of a Midget hockey team was the equivalent of today's Bantams. Be that as it may, on important games, the Ladies' Skate-Room door sign was covered over and *Visitors* papered over it. The Men's Skate-Room door sign was changed to read *Public Room* also *No-Smoking* was strictly enforced for the duration of the game. On a cold day, so many fans tried to get into that room, it was almost impossible to do. Consequently, a kind of informal rotation took place; Captain Jack, or his designate, would, from time to time, poke their head into the room through the door and holler, out to the warmed up: "Please move outside and let some others in."

When we arrived with the equipment, we found the Captain was busy putting up extra wall hangers—there being no team lockers. As a precaution, he attached a brand new hasp and padlock on the door.

"No hooligans are going to just walk into this room," he said, satisfied with his handy work.

The town Constable had come along with two team officials to oversee the transfer of equipment. During the actual game, the Constable monitored the team rooms, locking them up at his discretion. Blair and I made certain that the Constable would not mistake any of our actions as being that of hooligans. The two of us dragged in the heavy bag containing the goalie pads trying to figure out, largely by feel, what the pads might be like. We also thought that because of the weight, these pads had to be something special because they had the bulk, but not the weight, of the hometown team pads. We intended to pass this important information along to either Whizzer or Turk McKenzie. The bundle of Hockey sticks was CCM just like the Tigers. The rest of the gear, they too packed in canvas duffel bags, did not lend any information as to quality or actual colour of their team uniforms. It was only a rumour, but word had it that the sweaters and stockings of the Edmonton Royals team were maroon; but, as I have said, we were not able to check this out. After we received the customary "Good job boys," from Captain Jack we headed home, speculating, as we went on our team's chances of making it a good series. In truth, we were not at all certain that the Tigers could win against an Edmonton team; for it was common knowledge the overall calibre of the Tigers did not likely match that of the Royals. But, win or lose, we didn't want to see our boys embarrassed because of the superior play of their opponents. Aside from seeing the hockey sticks, we had also caught a quick look at the Royals' skates. Every pair had been Doust Specials with tendon guards and protected toes.

"Must have cost a real bundle," Blair exclaimed and I concurred mouthing the same words to emphasis the opinion. "And they looked practically all new too," he added, causing us to wonder what kind of team could actually afford to fit each of its members with brand new skates in one year.

"Very rich!" was our consensus.

It was difficult to come up with anything to comprehend the buying of that many skates in one season. My skates, as were Blair's, had been bought second hand at Rafferty's and we could only think of two people our age who had gotten new ones for Christmas, although my mother had said dad was going to try and do it for me next year.

We parted at my place, from where Blair continued down the street to the end of the block. Our plan was to convince our respective parents to allow us to go down town for a saunter after supper. I thought that my parents would allow it because I would be going with Blair who was older. Normally, we did not go there in the evening hours unless we had a specific errand to run. Not that it was all that exciting; but you never knew what might turn up, which according to my mom was exactly the point.

8

We were given permission to go down town that Friday however, we still had to observe the nine o-clock curfew. We didn't waste any time, for we wanted to try and get a good look at the Royal team members. In addition, we hoped to get a chance to say hello to a few of their players as they took to the ice for the pre-game practise. The practise was closed to the public but we thought, since we were practically rink staff, that Captain Jack would let us into the rink. He was having none of it! Our game day jobs carried no special status. We had already put in the wood and water supply, as I have mentioned, and, as far as the Captain was concerned, there was no need for us to be there. We were to find this out only after we had hurried along in time for the Royals' ice-time to begin—seven until eight thirty—after which our own Tigers then took to the ice. Clearly, we were going to have to wait until the actual game next day.

The actual start of the game next day was for one o'clock. The time selected was to allow for pre-game shopping for district farm families who would then be able to leave for home smartly after the game—enough travel time to make it home for the evening chores. The local stores closed their doors for about two hours and possibly longer if the game ran into overtime. In part, it had to do with whether or not the merchant was a hockey fan. There were, however, those few who could not divorce themselves from the chance of a little commerce so; to make it fair for all, the council passed a special mandatory two-hour closing for all businesses. The decree was made necessary because of those few merchants who wouldn't close for anything other than legal holidays. As luck would have it, we did meet up with a few hockey players leisurely strolling from downtown to the rink. One, an angular fellow with blond hair and an engaging smile, spoke to us right off without even waiting for an introduction.

You boys hockey players by chance?" he asked.

"Yeah well sort of," I responded thinking that if he meant in the same calibre, we were not; even Blair who was starting to get some height, could not be mistaken for a Junior B. Still I did not want to stretch a point. Blair, who himself was one tier up—Midgets—answered the query in about the same fashion.

"Are you any good?" he continued and, with out waiting for a reply, went on to ask about the Turnbull Tigers. "Any good players on the Tiger team?"

"Got some goal scorers?" asked a stocky fellow who we recognized as the goalie.

"Some are," I said.

"Only some?" the blond player spoke up.

"Well lots of the guys can score," Blair piped up, "And wait 'till you come up against Whizzer Jackson and Busher MacLean."

"Whizzer? Busher? What kind of names are those?" said the Blond.

"I suppose Whizzer is a whiz? Is that it? Busher? Stand for Bush league?"

He looked innocent and I knew he was baiting me, but I could not help but to respond, with a vigorous defense, that continued to the last block before the rink. Main Street was only four blocks long so mercifully that conversation was not for long.

"See you at the game Kid," said the Blond, still the main spokesman.

Captain Jack greeted the team, acknowledging us with an, "All right boys let these gentlemen by and I'll see you tomorrow."

He closed and hooked the entrance gate behind the last player.

We were left now with three options: go home early which we did not wish to do; go to the Friday night movie but first have to get permission from home; thirdly, shinny up a pole and drop down onto the roof to watch the proceedings, from there, but only, if we were quiet, and also, provided we stayed away from the team rooms where Captain Jack would be able to detect our presence. Even so, one false step on the shiplap roofing boards and it would be all over. The boards distributed sound like a drum head and the single layer of rolled roofing covering them over only added to the effect.

To be honest, the buildings and roofed over spectator areas were little more than unpainted sheds, yet because of their uniqueness, a source of some local pride. Years earlier, a town visionary, long before our time, had seen the rink as a profit maker and in a time of plenty convinced the powers that be that, unlike most other facilities in rural Alberta, Turnbull's rink would have an outer wall. This was an enclosure designed to make ticket sales possible instead of relying upon passing of the hat for revenue. Of course, ordinary games—Bantam teams and the like—didn't draw a crowd anyway so ticket sales were out of the question. The whole structure can be likened to crude scaled down version of a big city football stadium. The walls also kept out winds and nonpaying fans. I expect, if memory serves, not more than two hundred people could get in at one time and then that would be standing room only.

Even so, for special games or tournaments, even Midgets and Juveniles were allowed to charge a modest flat rate as a fund raiser but customarily only gate charges were made for play-off games. The charge, man women or child-over twelve was always twenty five cents a head.

In contrast, the money raised for Bantams and Pee Wees was done by mothers putting on Bean Suppers or perhaps an afternoon tea with a raffle of some sort added on. What ever amount of money raised, it provided for team sweaters, pucks, goalie pads and the like. Sticks were the player's responsibility but Goal nets—always hand me downs from Senior Teams—were supplied by the town and kept in shape by Captain Jack who was forever repairing them.

Tomorrow's game would have top netting for the goal areas, something Blair and I noted as we crept cautiously up the roof. We were not worried about being seen because of the glare created by a full string of rink lights—not just the recreational set. And, if one can imagine, sets of clear 150 watt light bulbs, about six to a string, strung from post to post about twelve feet over the ice surface, you will get the idea of what they were like. Five sets in all: one over center ice, two sets hung over and across blue lines, and the final two, strung in a line that passed above each goal crease. All five sets used only for actual games. Three being the norm for recreational skating and younger kids practises. Even Captain Jack admitted that there were considerable savings to be had by using only three strings of lights, and on moon light nights, why, they were hardly needed at all. Something that my pals and I knew all about because on spring nights, when the season closed and the rink locked up, we would crawl up over the roof and gain access to the rink. More exactly, we would boost one of our fellows up and over while the rest of us waited at a back gate to be unlocked from within. We took great pains to slip in unnoticed by any authority, principally the town's policeman and council members who would be obliged to order us out; notifying parents as well, who usually knew where we were in any case. Our village, being small, made it unlikely that the young could go unnoticed for long. Upon reflection, I think we were tacitly ignored by authorities until a complaint was made—often some childless citizen, the likes of Mrs. Smith-Jones or the widow McNab who seemed always suspicious of youth playing behind closed walls, hockey rinks and other such rendezvous.

And, because ours was a mixed group of boys and girls their suspicious minds seemed to work overtime. In our case, nothing untoward, we played a modified shinny game sans skates, hockey sticks or pucks. We did not use pucks for good reason, one they created too much noise and we wished anonymity; secondly, none of the group actually owned a real puck.

Pucks, carefully horded by the clubs, appeared only at practise or during games. As to *The Big Game* there would be no shortage of pucks. Rafferty's supplied them for all play-offs games for which they got a letter of thanks in the local paper as well as a public announcement before the game started.

If a puck flew over the boards or even out of the rink the public was expected to hand them back. No souvenir pucks to be had in those days and if any kid, like the time Paddy kept a puck, pretended that he had just found it out on the street everybody knew that this was not so and wouldn't let the culprit use it even for shinny out on the road. Moreover, there was a fair return for a finder if, as sometimes happened, a wild shot went up and over the roof areas or end boards. Then a small cadre of kids, waiting outside and often watching the game half-way up the extended roof support poles, would scramble onto the shed roof top then drop onto the road, there retrieving the puck before scurrying around to the back rink door. The finder let into the rink and also usually allowed to stay inside free of charge for the remainder of the game and was also rewarded with a five cent piece.

This time, however, we made our stay on the roof short as we did not want to risk the embarrassment of being caught nor did we want to jeopardize our jobs for the big game itself.

Our timing was fortuitous, as Captain Jack's nephew, Todder Simpson and Brady Jackson did get caught and threatened with a One Week Holiday if they didn't hurry home right away. They looked accusingly at us as they passed by on the street. We felt a little smug about it all, even satisfied at having gotten a glimpse of the Royals in action.

We had another good reason for leaving; my mom would have hot chocolate and also the radio on when we arrived home. Just in time to settle down for us to sit with my folks and listen to Lux Presents Hollywood. On that night we knew it was a Western starring Jimmy Stewart in Lux Theatre's adaptation of 'Destry Rides Again'. This we were not going to miss even if the Royals were on ice.

I really liked James Stuart's style the best. Blair, on the other hand, favored John Wayne. When the play was over Blair had to hurry along to meet the 8.30 curfew imposed by his parents. During the summer when it was light outside long into the evening we both could stay out unaccounted for until the Town's nine-o'clock curfew sounded. After that time anyone under age sixteen would be sent home; the only exception being if you attended the seven o'clock picture show—running usually until nine—after which you were supposed to be seen hurrying straight for home. Anyone caught detouring was in for trouble. Of course being out with your parents or another adult negated all the rules. Saturday night, when the stores were open until ten thirty, was another exception; but, it was generally understood that you had to have some business to stay out beyond the nine-o'clock curfew. The likes of Mrs. Smith-Jones would inform your parents if you didn't—you couldn't be seen just running around town making a nuisance of yourself.

9

On the morning of the game, I could hardly make it past my morning chores. My task was to clean out the overnight accumulation of wood ash from both cook stove and parlour heater, followed by bringing in our daily supply of wood, and lastly, hauling pails of fresh pumped water from a neighbour's well, then pulling the load, oh so carefully, home on my *Red Flyer* sled. The fact that father had recently started talking about getting a well of our own, as early as next year, of little consolation on that morning. Actually, my father had been saying this for several years now so neither mother nor I truly believed his stated good intentions.

In truth, few homeowners of the day were water well owners; money required to do it just too hard to come by. That was something no one had to explain to me. During weekdays, I didn't mind doing chores, but on Saturdays ... well it was different because, like washday Monday, extra water needed for our ritual Saturday night baths—whether there was a hockey game or no hockey game. I remember wishing that my mother would 'just this once' make an exception. Not that I actually disliked the ritual, but couldn't, on 'this day of days', could it not have been put off until Sunday or even Monday? It was a plea that fell upon deaf ears. And so, it was my fate to haul extra water right at the time my buddies were undoubtedly already down at the rink. Eventually, I got the job done, flew out the door of the house on the run, hollering that I would be home promptly at noon for lunch.

The episode with Grandad Cade and coming late for my own birthday neither forgotten nor quite forgiven by my mother.

Mother needn't have worried about my homecoming, because on this day I expected Captain Jack to promptly lock the rink doors at noon and go home to take his lunch. Other days, he sometimes did take along a sandwich and a jar of soup, which he heated in an old dipper hanging just above the Quebec heater. But on this Saturday, the bright sun and warm air made the lighting of a stove redundant. Even the rink ice was showing signs of starting to melt under the bright sun, so it was not difficult to ascertain that firewood was not needed for the dressing rooms, although water would be in big demand. Consequently, I actually had little to do prior to the game. Nevertheless, I was ready to lend a hand should there be any late developments, of whatever nature. I hurried to the rink hoping to be there by nine thirty before the end of the flooding. It was done and over with and I found him relaxing with his pipe. The worry now was as to how well the ice would hold up. Apparently, the Captain had arrived at seven in the morning when the air still registered below freezing temperatures. At least, he explained, the ice would be smooth and solid at the south end for as long as it was shaded from the sun.

"Might even make it to game time," he speculated.

His major concern, at this point and time, was about the north end, which, he was sure, would be wet as early as the second period for, at that time, the sun would be at its zenith.

"Bunch of dam fools should have had the game at night if they expected me to give the boys good ice," his voice edged with frustration, knowing the game would be played on an inferior ice surface. He was right about that, but the Council had to weigh the chances of getting optimum gate as opposed to playing on poor ice.

"Be the same for both teams," the Mayor had countered when advised of the risk. "Might even be to our boys advantage should the Edmonton boys be a faster team."

This was something I had not imagined, for as far as I was concerned, Whizzer Jackson and my cousin Busher were the fastest men on ice in our league and I didn't think you could get much faster than that. Still, the Mayor's words inserted a shade of doubt into this comfortable idea. I had lingering doubts, even as the Captain and I sat soaking up the morning sun. It was a nice lazy feeling and soon my thoughts drifted quite away from hockey and on to another warm day when street hockey had held no appeal. On a similar warm spring day, I had dug my Red Flyer from out beneath a snow bank, found a buddy and the two of us headed off to the sleighing trails, our own sleighs dragging behind, to look for any friendly, home bound, farmer with a team and bobsled. Not, I hasten to add, the bobsleds of modern times; the kind that go zipping down a mountainside at hair raising speeds. These were outfits drawn by light draft horses and not propelled by gravity. Sometimes, we caught rides behind the faster cutters, but mostly we tailed behind bobsleds. A bobsled was a four-runner rig split into two in the front, two in the back. The front-runners, used for steering, swivelled and as well as being the end, to hitch the horses. A complete rig consisted of two sets of steel covered runners connected, back to front, by a coupling pole that was attached at both ends to wood and iron devices called *hounds* upon which a set of *bolsters* were fitted, each having a pair of hickory stakes inserted to hold in the wagon box. The wagon gear itself was an ingenious combination of wood and iron akin to but unlike the running gear of an automobile.

In early spring and late winter, it was common to see the rigs without a box for the driver who, most likely, would be hauling his load of rails to sell in town as the next seasons' supply of firewood for a buyer. We looked for the rail-haulers because we knew that a good operator would try to make two trips into town all in one day. That meant we could catch an early ride out of town with one team and then catch a ride back with some other team a little later in the day. If it looked like a slow day, we were careful to ride out of town no further than we were willing to walk back. The uncertainty of it was also part of the attraction. On this day, I could tell right off that it would not be a good day for rides.

On this, the Saturday of the big game, hardly any farmers were heading home early. The vast majority had timed their arrival to give the wives and kids time to do the weekly grocery shopping while their men, sometimes with sons in tow, headed to the various stores where feed, hardware, harness repairs and lumber could be found. Also a good many teamsters would, often as not, stop in for a ten-cent beer at the hotel principally if they were German Lutherans, Anglicans, Catholics or no affiliation—coffee in the restaurant if you had an affiliation with the Evangelical Church or were United Church and had Methodist leanings. Even Smith-Jones (a United Church stalwart) was known now and then to slip in—most often when his wife was away visiting—enjoying, then, the company of three old-country gentlemen who continued with the habit of dropping into the *Village Pub.* Unfortunately, Turnbull's was nothing more than the infamous *Canadian Beer Parlour.* Still, this small group enjoyed their daily morning glass, unfailingly just after the ten o'clock opening. This illustrious threesome consisted of Judge Whittaker, creamery owner Lars Jensen, and the baker—whose name I have now forgotten, for I have been away too long. Although, he had moved on even before I myself did. I think perhaps that he was a Dutchman. Whether or not many of the rail haulers stopped at the parlour on this particular day, once they had unloaded, I do not know. I do know that most traveled to town alone, riding high on their loads and then straddling between the stakes on the journey back. I think the family men amongst the drivers, for the most part, chose not to quench their thirst, leaving that to another day when the whole family might come to town either by cutter or with their hauling boxes re-installed. I should add, that only those who had largely uncut wood lots were able to derive cash from their land clearing. We liked the rail-haulers because they were usually in a cheerful mood when hauling and ever ready to slow down enough to let you hitch a ride with your sleigh. One or two sporty types even decked out their team with sleigh bells. Indeed, many financially better-fixed farmers added the bells simply to show off their best when coming to town. Sleigh bells ringing certainly added to the growing festive mood of the village. The upcoming game fomented an unusually cheerful and friendly mood amongst the populace. It was something to be savoured and talked about, an undefined way of rejuvenating body and soul now that the end to a long hard winter was in sight. "Spring just around the corner!" could be heard in greeting from many of Turnbull's citizens whenever the sun shone and the temperature rose. People even had to wait to be seated at the Chinaman's, which is how active the village had become.

Some of the hockey crowd was gathering at the ticket office by the time I arrived, even though it was a full forty-five minutes before the two teams were scheduled to take to the ice, which gives you an idea of the excitement being generated. All the while, Captain Jack resisted all pleas to open the outside rink doors intent, as he was, on having everything ship shape.

His ice, in particular, despite the warm temperatures, lay in pristine beauty. The blue lines and face off circles freshly painted and gleaming beneath a clear glaze of ice. Captain Jack must have either stayed late after the practise sessions or he had gotten up terribly early.

I reasoned that he had stayed late, probably not getting home until after midnight as there were a few trouble spots starting to show up. I also knew that George Trefiak, a young section hand, who sometimes helped with ice making, had arrived after he had come off shift and had been busy diverting runoffs dripping over some of the rink roof sections adjacent to the northwest goal end. When I arrived, George was, by this time, shovelling scoops of snow onto the ice in an effort to soak up the excess water which when allowed to freeze could be shaved smooth, using a homemade ice tool of the Captain's making. Once the ice appeared level to the Captain's discerning eye, George then shovelled snow back onto the ice as a cover. There it would remain until a few minutes before the two teams took their respective pre-game skates.

"Told them they should play at night this time of year. But, as usual they don't listen." Captain Jack repeated this statement of the night before just to let George know that he had registered a complaint. George's friends would then also know, and so there would be no blame put on the Captain for the quality of the ice. This was a ritual with the Captain any time ice condition was mentioned within his hearing, never failing to get off a shot at the Council. Limiting him finally, to the flat statement that it should have been played at night because ice doesn't melt in the dark, was his analysis.

I set to work replenishing the water buckets and did some tidying up in the dressing rooms. Because it was getting so warm out, the Captain told me not to bother with a wood supply.

"Maybe see that there is kindling available for another day if you have time. If not don't worry about it."

Blair arrived a bit late, just as I was filling my last bucket at the pump room, so not getting a chance to speak to one and other, we simply exchanged one handed high signs. I carried on pumping water and he disappeared with a shovel in hand. I was using the handle rather than the pump engine as the pump jack and engine had been detached. There would be no need to flood the ice between periods on this day! I stalled in the pump shack for a few moments, just because I liked the wonderful sturdy smell of hard water taken from a shallow dug well that had an unending flow of water. It was of a quality deplored by housewives on wash days, but which, all the same, had a refreshing taste and had the unique quality of making ice as hard as rock. Turnbull's ice was slick and fast, not at all like the ice made with the water used at Clear Vista. That water, which was soft, and on the alkaline side, made ice that was decidedly slower if not having a downright gritty character to it.

The last two buckets were for the Tigers' dressing room; where most of the players had already dressed and were ready to go by the time I arrived. Not unexpected, my cousin Busher had not yet laced up his skates and was just sitting there, leaning back in his relaxed style, waiting until the last moment to tighten them up.

"Hurts my feet if I get them on too soon," was all he would say, while being kidded about being last man ready. Then, Busher didn't worry too much, about what was said to him on or off the ice.

"Stop the man and they don't get to shoot the puck," was his spoken philosophy.

Whizzer Jackson, on the other hand, had an intense look, a quick smile, and flashing eyes, which, it was said, got the attention of most every lady he ever met. Looking back, I think that these attributes were probably his best personal assets, but being of an age where girls were not of major importance in life, I probably never realized the kind of masculine charm Whizzer actually had. Busher was a contrast in many ways, friendly, reserved smile, a big framed sandy-haired man; Whizzer dark haired and only medium sized. While Busher was pretty much as you saw him on or off the ice. Whizzer, off ice, was polite and mild mannered. On ice, more than one big man learned that if you tangled with Whizzer Jackson there was a price to pay in any attempt to intimidate him. Moreover, Whizzer was so elusive on ice that he hardly ever took a body check that he didn't instigate himself.

This was not a time for small talk and as soon as I set the pails down, I left because you could feel the teams' nervous tension, their individual minds working on how to handle the next sixty minutes. Outsiders, even the chore boys, were not welcome. Turk began his pre-game instructions as I exited. I knew by the way he tugged at his red moustache that he was as keyed up as any member of the team.

The Edmonton Royals were just skating on to the ice when I emerged. They looked invincible, and their practise skates were fast and smooth, going one way around the ice smartly turning as one then reversing direction for another turn around, stopping finally in a line at their own Blue line. About the only thing in which the teams were alike was in the fact that each club had blue as the main colour, only the hue, in reality, different from one and the other. It was as if, you were seeing home team, road team, jerseys of the same club; not that at the time anyone knew of a team owning two different sets of uniforms—not in our league at any rate. The sweaters were the only standard item worn by each Tiger member. Pants were a mix of colours, mostly khaki, two or three wore black and, I think, there was one white pair worn by a forward whose name escapes me now. Cousin Busher and Tucker Munroe—a junior with big time ambitions—both had new style pants with kidney protectors. Stockings, well they were indeed a hodgepodge, somewhat alike but coming from three different teams and quite unlikely bought from the same supplier, and even less likely to all be bought in the same year. But, despite this lack of dress continuity, they managed to look good in spite of the inadequacies.

Once the warm-up was over, the two teams lined up and the Mayor made a little speech at center ice with Carl Gassing having the honour of dropping the ceremonial puck. Immediately after the Mayor and Carl then escorted to an area behind the team box, where a few extra benches had been placed and reserved for the event. Myself, I managed to squeeze a place next to the home team box in the space taken up by the ice cleaners. Blair squeezed in beside me and Captain Jack, where we took up a position just off the chicken wire screen—back of the north goal and close to the east side gate. Everything was set and everyone present quieted down in anticipation of the first face off.

10

From the moment Sandy Thompson dropped the game starting puck right down to the final minute, there was hardly a person in the crowd who didn't give that game his or her undivided attention. In fact, some local citizens had not stopped talking about it as late as Easter when the up-coming baseball season was the preferred subject for sports talk and hockey just a memory.

Nothing at all startling happened in the first five minutes of play as the two teams felt one and other out; although, it became apparent that our third line was not as good as the Royals' third string.

To compensate, Turk McKenzie double shifted Busher and his partner Leon Shultz whenever possible. Whizzer, with line mates Bo Beales and Jimmy Brody were as good as expected but did not have things their own way, being up against a tough disciplined Royals' line. Still, there was no change on the Tigers' second string: Dutch Jamieson, Tucker Monroe, and Joe Schmall—a junior playing for the Clear Vista View Intermediates. He was only a pedestrian player who, on occasion, could be sparked by Tucker Monroe. Tucker was, himself, unpredictable or entirely predictable depending upon whether or not you were a fan of his raw talent.

The friendly blond, who had talked to us the night before, had a name, which we soon discovered was Duchak. Duchak, a centre, did not have the quick hands that Whizzer was blessed with. Consequently, Whizzer had the edge in winning face-offs. Nevertheless, Duchak, once in motion, was impossible to catch; he was also rugged and not the least afraid to lay on the body. Moreover, his wingers did a sound job of back checking. The Whizzer line had to be very careful when playing against the line to make no mistakes. It became apparent very quickly into the game, that there would be no easy goals against the line. In fact, the Tigers were to get few actual shots on goal the entire first period although once, just once, they came close.

First off, Whizzer slowed the tempo of play with a dazzling display of stick handling. To the uninitiated, he gave the appearance of being an indecisive fumbler surprising those watching, by suddenly laying on a deek that sent his wingers over the Royals' blue line creating a two on three. Bo Beales went full steam across the goalmouth taking the right defenseman with him. Jimmy Brody hung back forcing the second defenseman to put a move on Whizzer who slide the puck through his legs catching Jimmy on the fly for a timed, patented play that produced a shot on goal—a flipped puck high on the net. The crowd went wild until a few noticed that the goal judge had not called it a goal. Sandy Thompson skated over to check with the goal judge who had neither raised his hand nor turned on the red light. The crowd groaned in disappointment when Sandy indicated no goal. I was close enough to hear "hit the goal post" as the lineman skated by the bench to give an explanation. Not everyone accepted this including old man Benson who continued to gripe and cry foul. Then he, and others of the same ilk, always complained whenever a ruling went against the hometown. In this case, there was no serious objection, but the Royals did have a scare put into them; so we all knew it was going to be only a matter of time before the Tigers scored.

Even so, it took more than a near miss to upset the Royals style of play. Surprisingly, it was their third string, not the first or second, that caused a stir amongst the Turnbull fans. Moments after our best and only chance at getting on the score board, their third line which, to this point, showed mostly flash, changed tactics and succeeded in tangling up play at center ice—they dispsy-doodled about going nowhere, but retaining absolute control of the puck. You would have thought that they were in our end working on a power play the way they positioned themselves. It wasn't until Busher stepped out of his defensive role, and moved in on the play, that the Royals were stopped, by this time well into Tiger territory. The Royals stymied by Busher's quick action appeared to be in retreat and the puck carrier made what looked to be a forced panic pass. Then, just as the receiving Royals player seemed the most desperate he made another pass so casual it looked like a throw away. It wasn't. The winger made as if he was being forced back into the direction of his own goal; then, suddenly, got off a harmless looking backhanded pass. The puck shot waist high past Busher, when it then bounced off the boards and into the Tigers' corner. His two Royals line mates, right on cue, turned away from the flow of play and took off the instance they heard the crack of hockey stick striking puck. A rehearsed move caught both Tigers and their fans totally and absolutely by surprise. Shooting the puck blindly into a corner and then chasing after it is today a commonplace, but it was not back then. A player shooting the puck blindly into a corner for his mates to chase and then fight for puck control was something neither our team, nor our fans, had ever experienced. Unexpectedly, there it was, a new move orchestrated with startling effectiveness. The Royals' left wing simply rushed in, picked up the puck, leaving the Tigers, disorganized, and goalie Sid Simpson unprotected and at the mercy of the full forward line. It looked like a goal against. No one who saw was ever sure whether it was just Sid's quick hands—he was the best hardball catcher every produced locally—or quick hands aided by the soft ice that saved the day. Then again, the shooter faltering for but a second failed to get off the expected quick wrist shot. As I have said, Sid, appearing to have little chance, managed a gloved save while going down, puck in hand, and rolling over on his belly—his action thereby forcing a face off.

The first period, seconds to go, ended scoreless to the delight and vocal appreciation of the fans loud applause for the two teams as they skated off to begin the first intermission.

The second period was also scoreless, and, while entertaining, only two memorable incidents that occurred. One, I am sorry to report was a display of poor sportsmanship on the part of our own Tucker Monroe. Tucker, an emotional player of promise, but too often took to being a one-man show and much given to grandstanding. He was built like an early day Hull—take either Bobby or Brent along with that famous smile of the older Hull and you get some idea of the way he looked. He was rugged, fast, and not quite the player he thought he was. I doubt if anyone on the ice that day was faster than Tucker—not even Duchak. Yet, Duchak had an advantage, as he was a disciplined junior player who knew his own strengths; also, I expect, he played much the same way each time out. Tucker had few of these attributes.

As the Captain put it, "When that boy is hot he is hot and the rest of the time he can be just bloody awful!"

Most of the time, especially during this game, he was just awful. Once, when his line was against the Duchak line, with instructions to try and keep that line off the score board, Tucker went on a wild one man charge that ended with the Edmonton defense taking away the puck, then quickly making a long pass out to a forward, who was suddenly given easy entry over the Tigers own line.

Tucker's action had negated Turk McKenzie's attempt to get on the score board by double shifting the Whizzer line, taking home team last change advantage against a weaker opponent—the Tigers, being the home team, had that privilege.

The tactic was not going as expected; at first the Duchak line was put off its smooth play largely because Tucker put a couple of after the whistle hits on Duchak who seemed impervious to this action only displaying a little smile when Sandy Thompson warned Tucker after the second hit. Of course, Tucker made a great public display of innocence. Sandy disdained to argue the point and blew his whistle for a face off. I think Duchak's little smile was important because Tucker failed in both attempts to knock Duchak off his skates which seemed to rile Tucker up some more. You could tell that something was going to happen despite Sandy Thompson's warning.

Still, despite his shortcomings, Tucker's tactics had some of the desired effect. His third string line even getting some scoring chances against the Royals' first line as their polished play had a little of the edge rubbed off. Pay off came on the third shift, with only minutes to go, when the Tigers seemed to lose their earlier caution and sensing that the Royals were not invincible put together a nice play. It started when Busher got off a long pass to Barney Plummer who sent our two third string wingers over the line and defenseman Leon Shultz quickly up to the Royals' Blue line. Just two quick passes had sent Tucker breaking in. Tucker, now double shifted, after Dave Fisher took a puck on the ankle, shot a sizzler to the top right of the net. It was going in for sure but ... the "but" being the Royals' goalie who stuck out an arm knowing there was a price to pay for doing so. Play was immediately stopped! Despite a leather elbow pad, the rifling shot had rendered his arm numb. Every one in that rink reacted as if they too were sharing his intense pain. The assistant coach, first on the ice, immediately signaled the bench to send out Doc McIntyre. A fracture seemed likely. Fortunately, it was not and the upshot was only a five-minute delay until feeling came back into the arm. Once the pain subsided, enough for the Royals' goalie's return to net minding the game was back on. Turnbull fans then gave the Royals' player a big hand and as he in turn had given them something to talk about for weeks after—the brilliant stopping of a certain goal.

It had been a moment to be cherished—a cleverly engineered shot on goal by our third string. It was a shot that could easily have been the game winner but for the courage and brilliance of a goal tender not known to us until that day. As the period ended, about three minutes to go, I should think, both teams were showing signs of fatigue. The once glistening ice, dulled by the brilliant February sun, was pooling in the corners and at the shadeless north end. Hockey purists were muttering disapproval "... I told them so," could be heard in pockets of discontent. Not too loudly, for they also knew that this game had drawn the biggest out-of-town crowd of the winter and local businesses would benefit greatly.

Then, in the dying minutes of the second period, an ugly incident occurred which I regret to say was caused by one of our own. I can only recount from others what happened because, being water boy, I had hurried into the dressing rooms before the period's end busily replenishing the players room water buckets and, as well, made myself available to run errands. It was a job I liked because it put me right on the scene where important off ice decisions was made. I was also the envy of many of my peers because of this 'insider' position going with the job. So moments from the period end, I was heading for the dressing rooms passing by Captain Jack who was himself, not aware of the incident, conferring with game officials as to whether or not he should try a light flooding of ice before the final period. However, considering the blazing sun and melting ice a consultation seemed just a tad ludicrous. Nevertheless, the committee having precious else to do could say that everyone involved had considered all the aspects.

In the midst of all this soul searching—which the Captain, blank faced as they come, patiently listened to—came a mixed sound of boos and some cheering. The cheering for some reason stopped but some booing continued, the sound of which caused the delegation to turn to the ice. Collectively, we expected to witness the aftermath of some Edmonton player's mayhem or act of poor sportsmanship. Why else was the crowd showing displeasure, I thought. A fan at the screen in front turned to explain what had happened.

"That Monroe boy again," explained the fan, who, to my surprise, was none other than Mr. Smith-Jones. The one man in town I had never considered a fan. "Most unsportsmanlike, he tripped the Edmonton lad right in front of the net looked like he would have scored a goal too. He had our man beaten. That young Cock is about as sportsmanlike as Lee Fong's bantam rooster."

Jack Fisher standing nearby exploded in disgust. "Got a penalty shot I presume?"

"Some dispute over that," continued Smith-Jones. "Sandy wasn't on top of the play. I think he thought it might have been bad ice as well. He did give the Monroe boy a two minute so the Edmonton team seems satisfied. Have to finish the penalty in the third in any case."

"If that sun keeps on beating down we may not get much farther than halfway through the third." Captain Jack observed turning to Smith-Jones, a bit of 'I-told-them-so' in his voice.

"Right you are Jack," responded Smith-Jones surprising me further in that he used the Captain's first name as if they were on intimate terms. Just one more surprise from the adult world I thought, getting some further revelations as Smith-Jones continued to talk about Tucker Monroe. "That boy could be a dashing good hockey player if he ever learns to keep his head about him ... amazing raw talent there," he said, confusing me even more because he seemed to know much more about hockey than I had ever imagined, moreover Captain Jack nodded his head in agreement. Captain Jack actually agreeing with someone other than himself was to say the least something.

"Changed the call," announced, Smith-Jones suddenly turning his attention back to the ice where the final minute of the period was unfolding. "Penalty shot coming up," he added. This piece of action no one wanted to miss and I had a hard time trying to squeeze my small sized frame into a vantage point. When I did manage, it was my luck to be standing where the end boards stood higher. Even on tiptoes, I could not watch Duchak start a confident half circle for his drive down the ice. He swooped like a hawk; six feet from the circle, going to the glove side and made an amazing cut hard to the right and, in the same motion, flipped a backhander at Simpson's stick hand. The hush was such that you could hear that puck from one end of the rink to the other as it banged the goal post and ricocheted in. The subdued fans looked on in disbelief. Even as the sound of the ringing puck noise stopped, Tucker Monroe's name could be heard muttered under the breath of the fans as they headed for the one lone skating room open to the public. The fans moved along, more out of habit, as it was not cold even though they had little chance of getting into the one small room assigned. The talk centered on "... that Duchak fella ... did you see that move?" The likes of which had not been seen since whenever someone could conjure up a similar happening factual or not. In the Royals' dressing room, there was jubilation.

"Well kid, haven't heard much from the Whizzer line of yours," said one of the players Blair and I had been in conversation with the night before. I had little to say in response, knowing that action not words was the only thing the home team needed now. "By the way," the player continued, "who was the clown tripped Duchak up and gave him a free ride?"

"Aw Monroe, Tucker Monroe," I responded, the words of Smith-Jones still in my head and embarrassed that the goal had been gotten in the manner in which it had.

"Monroe, huh ... too bad; if he took time to learn a few things, discipline being one, he could turn into a hell of a player. But then I don't suppose he ever will."

"Well right now I'm glad he hasn't learned temper control just yet." Duchak was smiling broadly and got briefly into the conversation.

"You ought to know Cracker." The big blond player joshed good-naturedly, giving me the suspicion that maybe Duchak's calm exterior hadn't always been.

I finished my chores as quickly as possible avoiding any further humiliation over the Tigers' lack of scoring power.

All Turnbull fans could now do was hope that the Tigers well-known talent for pulling things out of the fire would come to the fore during the third. It was unthinkable to me that they could not overcome a simple score of one to nothing. However, not everyone seemed to share my optimism including a gathering of fans, outside the Tiger dressing room, which I had to push through without spilling my bucket of water.

The spokesman for the bunch seemed to be a large tough looking man I did not know but heard him say 'my boy' a couple times. The tenor of the conversation had to do with the line-ups, causing me to realize the talker was likely the Clear View Junior's father. I had heard of him once before, during an overheard conversation my father had with Carl Gassing. It seems that the man, a political power on his own turf, was trying to use it on Turnbull officials. The gist of his discontent was that Mike Plommer was not, in his view, getting enough ice time much to the displeasure of the Clear View fans—Mike Plommer being Clear View's version of Whizzer Jackson. Simply put, they wanted their own hockey hero to be given the chance, "To win this game ..." The Clear View bunch was now demanding an audience with the coach. Carl Gassing met the delegation at the door and blocked their entry to the player's room.

"Now boys ... Coach is doing his best. We leave tactics to him." I heard him say, but the big man from Clear Water was having none of it. There were a few tense moments that ended suddenly when Turk McKenzie made his appearance.

"Mr. Plommer," he greeted and seemingly not surprised. There was an edge to his voice. Plommer, not quite up to Turk's stony eyed stare, lost his resolve muttering a few words about his son not playing enough his rational petering out as Turk continued to stare.

"Thank you very much Mr. Plommer for your concern. I'll take it into account." Turk then abruptly re-entered the team room and closed the door behind leaving Plommer slack mouthed, his audience over. Carl Gassing suggested politely that he go back to rink side and enjoy the game. Minutes later, the Tiger players began filing out giving the subdued Mr. Plommer no notice and forcing him to step aside. The interesting thing, I learned later, was that Mike Plommer Jr. himself was just grateful to be playing and just pleased to be in the company of superior players.

11

Whether or not the third period would run the full twenty minutes was now problematic. Captain Jack allowed only a light scrapping of the general ice surface followed by the repairing of the worst wet spots and ruts by smoothing them over with snow. Even so, despite his crew's efforts, working now under a high blazing spring sun, the results were mostly cosmetic. How long any of it would last was anybody's guess. In fact, water had started to pool along the entire length of the east side on up to the north end now occupied by the Tigers. Here again, Captain Jack had attempted to stem the wet by packing the worse skate cuts with snow. It was the best he could do, that and praying it might prevent any serious injury to the players.

Shortly into the period, it became apparent that Turk McKenzie was going to gamble on two lines doing the work. He created a mix of the second and third line players, using second-string centre man Tucker Monroe sparingly, double shifting Whizzer Jackson and relying heavily on the older, steadier players to keep the game even. It did take some of the excitement out of the game by doing so, but Turk knew the team's only hope was to limit the Royals' scoring chances and hope that the Tigers got a break. One advantage of the soft ice, was the fact that it took away the fast pace that the swifter Royals had set in the earlier going. The Royals soon found out that shooting the puck down the ice and chasing after it was no longer working in their favour and their organized breakaway attempts soon faltered. The last time the tactic was tried by the Duchak line, the big center placed his usually accurate pass just a might short on the east side and sent his winger sloughing on the north end ice like a champion barefoot water skier.

The Tigers, on the other hand, having experienced these conditions many times before, found the slower ice much to their liking. This, combined with the familiar smaller rink size, allowed them more game control than they had for the first two periods. The game became one of check, check, check.

Much to the Tigers liking, the game was beginning to resemble a Sunday afternoon shinny game bringing alive the Tigers and giving Whizzer more ice control. His style seemed to baffle his opponents. They couldn't just knock him down. If they did, somehow he no longer had the puck at the moment of impact causing the offending Royals player to take a penalty for his efforts. He was equally adept at tucking the puck in between an opposing player's feet and then retrieving it as he came circling around. If an opposing player tried a-clutch-and-grab, they picked up a holding or interference penalty because Whizzer never seemed to have possession of the puck at the time of the infraction. The Royals, not slow learners, ceased taking penalties but still Whizzer baffled them. Their defensemen next tried poke checking. Whizzer, anticipating, just dumped the puck over the line catching either Bo Beales or Jimmy Brody with a quick pass and a quick shot on goal. The crowd went wild each time it happened. Despite Whizzer's masterful displays, there were still no goals. Worse, time was running out.

The Royals, knowing time was now on their side, took to stacking four men on the blue line finally finding an effective strategy for stopping the Whizzer Jackson line. Whizzer, himself, soldiered tirelessly on enjoying himself, and taking only three personal time outs during the entire period.

With less than two minutes to go, Turk McKenzie called a time out, stopping play just outside the Royals' blue line. The conference at the bench was intense, Turk doing the talking and only the nodding of heads let the fans know that whatever the scheme to save the day was, both players and coach agreed. This also gave the beleaguered Royals a break; the Royals players skated unconcerned over to their own box, quite confident that they could hold the win. They had an air of quiet confidence as their own coach mapped out the defensive strategy. Even so, the matter seemed quite simple to Tigers' fans. We all knew that despite Whizzer's peskiness, the defending Royals continued to break up plays and if they failed, the Royals' net minder pulled off magnificent saves. At the other end, where ice conditions were even poorer, a Royals' rush on the mostly idle goalie made it easy for the shots to be turned aside. The Royals were unable to score another goal even as they tried to increase their lead. Eventually, and nearing the end of the period, the Royals' squad quit trying to score goals and instead concentrated on playing defensive hockey. Their strategy was to dump the puck quickly into the end zone then make a quick line change to insure that they always had fresh legs on the ice. It wasn't exciting hockey but it was paying off for the Royals.

Game almost at an end, the crowd quieted, resignedly awaiting the final whistle. To everyone's surprise, the line chosen for this last play was not the Tigers' number one line. It wasn't a combination that anyone would have guessed. Turk had decided to gamble: leading off with the unpredictable Tucker Monroe at left wing; Whizzer Jackson, of course, at center; Dutch Jamieson, instead of Bo Beales, at right. Turk was going for size. Both Dutch and Tucker were much bigger men than either Jimmy Brody or Bo Beales. Jimmy was sitting out the final, but Bo Beales, because of his speed, stayed and moved back to be floater. Turk's final move was to pull the goalie and set my cousin Busher MacLean and Leon Shultz on defense. Except for Whizzer and Bo Beales, these were the Tigers' biggest players. The Royals having already made a player change suddenly realized they were facing a formidable line-up but were too late to make any further player changes. The Tigers, because of home ice advantage, had the final change. It was a nice bit of generalship and the hometown crowd appreciated it. Another break, from our point of view, was that Tucker, put on wing, would not be facing Duchak who had had the best of him for most of the afternoon.

Sandy Thompson took his time, making certain that the linesman was positioned exactly on the blue-line so that he could see and immediately call any possible offside.

The puck was dropped and immediately whistled down. The crowd groaned because Whizzer had possession. Could he do it again? We held our collective breaths as the puck dropped, fairly this time. Whizzer did it again. In one of his patented moves, he deeked Duchak with what looked to be a backhand pass behind causing Duchak to rush ahead. Whizzer, instead, feinted to his own right side pulling and causing Duchak, and the Royals' right-winger to move out of position expecting to block a pass that did not come. Suddenly, Whizzer golfed the puck high over the blue line, sending Tucker Monroe flying into the corner with all his speed and raw talent. It was inspiring to watch, Whizzer had stolen that move right from the Royals' bag and they had not expected it. Much too late, their defense scrambled in after Tucker tangling themselves up as Tucker literally crawled over their backs and passed the puck smack out to the goal mouth where Busher and Leon Schultz were holding off against Duchak and his winger. The Royals' left-winger had a hold on Whizzer thinking he was the intended shooter. The entire rink of onlookers thought the same. Both the Royals and the crowd had assumed wrong. Bo Beales, the floater, was the intended man; accordingly, he stepped in all alone, picked up the pass and popped it in through the maze of players. It was beautiful! Cowbells rang, while fans cheered and hugged one another. Nobody, long after the game was over could remember having such a good time.

No overtime played, both Tigers and the Royals concurring with referee Simpson that what was going on now could hardly be called hockey. A few waggish fans took up a cry hollering out to give the players brooms and a ball following the announcement that the game had ended. The crowd, now in a carnival mood, cheered the suggestion. In truth, Broomball was a game for old men and high school girls. It was not hockey.

12

During the week after the game, the local citizens talked of and about the game to the point where most ran out of anecdotal tales to tell. Once this seemingly endless store of trivia, as expressed by the locals, had exhausted itself and talk became mundane—the excitement of it all wrung out—then their attention turned to *Artificial Ice* and Edmonton. The subject of artificial ice, to the uninformed, brought about considerable guessing as to just what it was and how it might be made. For instance, the arena, the reasoning went, had to be like a kind of giant hay barn. Just one big refrigerator-freeze pinioned several citizens.

Old Mr. Benson, for one, explained that it stood-to-reason that the building would have to be pretty much like being inside Jack Fisher's refrigerated meat cooler. Now that was an exciting idea, but being a little sceptical, we decided to consult with the one person in town who could verify such a claim. Therefore, as soon as school let out, we went off to Doc Rafferty's shop where we found the place not officially open but knew, if he was around, you could get in at the back door. As I related earlier, Doc Rafferty's was a kind of fix all repair shop. You could take your radio to Doc and he would test your tubes or if you had a cranky gas pump engine with a faulty magneto Doc could solve the magneto problem and he would do it without charge. Ring changes, valve grinds and the like as well as any other kind of engine work; that sort of job one took to Gassing's. Almost anything else you could think of: a faulty appliance cord, a bicycle needing a tune-up, a few new spokes needed in a bike wheel, a sign painted, or a poster made up; Doc Rafferty's was the place to go. One thing customers learned, was that you didn't want to be in a hurry to have the job done. Doc took his time but it was always quality work and, when he did charge, he didn't charge too much.

Doc as mentioned, was of independent means, a remittance man, and an educated man, although, there were no diplomas or the like displayed in his shop. Why he was called Doc I do not know; but I expect, it was because of his learned ways. He spent his time drinking, reading, repairing and inventing. Moreover, because he had an inventive mind, many locals believed he had to have been educated at some sort of technical or scientific school back in England. If so, he never alluded to it, offering no evidence whatsoever to support this thesis. Whatever his peculiarities, he had maintained a certain local respect for his person despite a certain amount of joking about his ways—although not in his presence. The front office door of Doc's place was customarily locked as he observed Thursday afternoon closure. Often he continued to work away at his private pursuits or he might tinker with some gadget or other. Then again, he might simply laze on his back, smoking cigarettes, and read pulp fiction. Judging by the periodicals scattered about his place, his tastes seemed to run mostly to the yarns of Ray Bradbury and the like. I knew of this habit because of the few times I delivered the Edmonton Bulletin for Arnold—an older boy who had contracted mumps. Doc was very uncommunicative on those occasions. This time, I could only hope we would not find him that way. Luck was with us, we could hear some activity in the back end of the shop. So we cut between Doc's and Burton's Hardware expecting to find him behind his lot. He was nowhere in sight and the paint-faded, double-hinged garage doors were closed. Even so, we figured he was inside. Because we didn't have the nerve to bang on the doors, we turned away to leave. Then, at that precise moment of our departure, a puff of exhaust fumes belched from a piece of iron pipe stuck through the end of the building. The double-hinged doors burst open and Doc hurled himself outside.

Once the smoke cleared, and Doc was through coughing, he explained that he was testing a very noisy gasoline engine of foreign design, which had backfired, causing an excess of exhaust fumes. He invited us into his shop once the air had cleared. We cautiously followed him back, watching as he reset the spark and again fired up the engine. This time the machine, the likes of which we had never seen, fired and began an erratic 'putt-putting.' Quite fascinated, we asked no questions; just stood and watched until it eventually ran out of gas. Something that did not take too long because the fuel system at that point consisted of a hand held one-quart mason jar fitted with a siphoning tube which he had fashioned from a bent piece of copper gas line. The fuel flowed from the jar into the engine in a rather uneven flow causing the engine to rev-up, sputter, and rev-up some more and when on the verge of stopping it would go again.

Had we questions to ask, they would not have been heard because the engine, without a muffler, was making quite deafening internal explosions. Although the engine looked nothing like its modern counterparts, Doc said it was designed to exhaust under water. The drive mechanism consisted of a simple open propeller shaft, which was then fitted to the inside hull of a boat. For try-outs and tuning, Doc mounted it on a pipe-work tripod straddling a five-gallon, grease pail filled with water, which supplied the engine's water jacket.

The engine itself was a design made to be used as an inboard and not, as mentioned, resembling a modern day boat motor. Nothing was enclosed. It had an open driveshaft and a heavy cast iron flywheel at the front; no safety features of any type on this two hundred pound behemoth, and no shielding of moving parts, unless the boat builder himself saw fit. Even for the thirties, it was a bit of an antique. Nevertheless, we thought it impressive despite the fact that it produced only four horsepower at full throttle. It simply looked large and very rugged which was enough for our unsophisticated minds.

Eventually, Doc was satisfied with the trial run. The gasoline in the jar had run out, causing the engine to sputter to a stop. Only then, were we finally able to broach the matter of artificial ice.

Doc Rafferty obliged, quickly setting us straight on the matter.

"Boys ..." he said in his precise English voice, "boys you have come to the right place. I shall sketch out a diagram for you."

We settled on each side of his drafting board as he drew. The drafting board itself, the only one in town—even the local newspaper did not have one—was quite exotic in our eyes. It was there, upon this board that he sketched out ideas and projects practical or fanciful. In short order he had drawn a schematic showing a maze of pipe work joined to an enormous compressor looking much like Gassing's tire compressor. Rafferty pointed that fact out to us as an aid towards understanding that part of the system. Even so, we did struggle with the idea of how gas can be compressed into liquid, if indeed that is what was forced into the pipes. The pipes were laid over a sand bed and flooded with water. The water cooled down because of the displacement of heat, eventually froze and turned into ice for the rink. That, he explained, was why it was termed *artificial-ice*. It was not the ice that was artificial we learned, but rather the way in which water was frozen was where the term *artificial-ice* came from.

The two of us did our best to soak in every sketched in detail of his diagrams. By the time we were through, we had become quite excited over what we had learned; after which, we hurried on home full of desire to display our newfound knowledge with schoolmates and family alike. We thought of ourselves as disciples and soon found out that, like those who spread words of enlightenment, most recipients did not care. "Is that so!" was too often the only response.

Even so, we were, ourselves, satisfied with having solved the puzzle of *artificial-ice*. Still, neither we nor anyone else had a solution to the problem of how to transport the Tigers to Edmonton for the game on their *artificial-ice*. Unlike the better-funded Royals, the Turnbull Tigers were either going to be individually out of pocket or having to relying upon private donors to fund their transportation. That in itself was one problem. Problem number two was a matter of a finding satisfactory ice time as the local ice was gone and there were only limited available ice times available at the Edmonton arena. Saturday night, at Edmonton, seemingly was the most freely available practise time. This posed a problem for most of the team's players as well as the coach and management staff because the group consisted largely of working men. The volunteer drivers faced the same dilemma; acerbated further by the fact that Turnbull was a Saturday Night Town. For the most part, they just could not afford to close up shop on a Saturday. Saturday, was the day that the area's district farmers came to town, looking for groceries, staples, hardware, also because they brought to town their saleable weekly supplies of eggs and cream. And, generally, they shopped locally for whatever essential needs the farm family might have. Saturdays, as well as for the twice a month Stockyard days, had the most importance for the merchants.

Sunday noon being the designated time for the game, it became a matter of whose, as much as how many, automobiles the committee could muster for the trek to the big city. Although a last minute push to fund transportation by rail did take place, it quickly died as soon as someone pointed out, to the ad hoc transportation committee, that passenger trains did not stop at Turnbull on Sundays nor did the Weigh Freight—a term given to the light freight haul and passenger train. Therefore, the mode of transportation had to be private vehicle. In those days, if you were wondering, rural bus transportation didn't exist; neither private hire nor regular run.

The problem was more than just the matter of finding willing automobile owners; it was also a matter of finding owners with automobiles capable of making the sixty-five mile run to Edmonton. Despite a considerable spring-like thaw taking place, driving conditions were still winter-like; travellers could expect overnight freezing temperatures and; as for the use of a snowplough, only the likes of the Aberhart highway got infrequent attention. Unfortunately, our village was not adjacent to it. Turnbull, like most of the small communities, had to fend for itself. In an emergency the County, with one truck and a cat, would use that equipment to bust open short distances of road. Generally, though, there was neither contracted work nor designated equipment for routine snow removal, which is why trains were so important in those days. Back to automobiles; first off in winter, as I have said earlier, few citizens bothered to keep their vehicles in running shape. Motoring, for most, ended from about the last week in November to mid-December, depending upon weather, and did not resume until about mid-March to April.

There were five possibilities: The Mayor's, Dodge Flat-Six, Gassing's four-door Ford V-8 Deluxe, Jack Fisher's dandy '32 Nash—which could at least handle four and perhaps five, if as Captain Jack put it "… only if you were close friends or lovers." True, Turk McKenzie did have a Model A-Ford, equipped with a rumble seat, but of a style out of the question for this time of year. Even so, as it did handle a pile of equipment, it was being considered. Doctor Monroe's 1934 Chevrolet was an outside possibility; but, as usual, it was in need of new tires. As likely, the Doctor himself would drive, no substitute driver would be needed. Smith-Jones would not drive because he and a woman with nursing skills always filled in while the Doctor was away. Moreover, so far, Smith-Jones had made no offer of his own vehicle. The Doctor's car also needed a valve job but Gassing thought it might do. Not too promising a caravan until Smith-Jones' McLaughlin-Buick, the most magnificent vehicle in town, was unexpectedly offered.

The news that it was being used caused quite a stir because no one could remember seeing it on the streets after the November 11th Armistice Day and then not until before March 17th, St. Patrick's Day. These two special days were benchmark days for our community just as were Valentines, Victoria Day, Dominion Day, Thanksgiving, Halloween, Christmas and New Years, in that order. These dates always commemorated by celebrations and, frequently, annual community dances with strict adherence as to sponsorship: WW1 Veterans on Armistice Day; Women's Institute, Valentines; and on down to the local Moose, Elks Club, and the like; each claiming ownership of a particular holiday event and dance. Other dances came about intermittently for such functions as weddings, or ball clubs needing to raise money, or simply because life had gotten a little tedious and some group thought to liven things up.

Back to the Buick: it was big, rugged, and powerful. Six big men could ride comfortably in it. It had eight in-line cylinders and purred like a kitten when it was driven. A showpiece, it rarely went anywhere. Moreover, few would have imagined it was going to go anywhere this time. Even so, a delegation of team officials had earlier sought out Smith-Jones who finally acquiesced.

"One thing for sure," volunteered Captain Jack, after hearing about the delegations visitation, "it'll be like pulling hen's teeth getting Smith-Jones to agree to it."

Much of what Captain Jack had to say was true enough for Smith-Jones was known as a penny-wise person having strict and separate allotments of his finances for business and pleasure. It took Carl Gassing to change his mind.

"Tell you what," he offered, "suppose I give Nick Thorpe the day off? Won't cost you a dime."

The offer allowed Smith-Jones to set aside all his fears and imagined ruination of his prized possession. He had been mulling it over for days, and delayed this decision until the last minute, hoping, somehow, to escape making a decision at all.

"Well that is generous of you, and I do support the team. Mind you I would not personally be going if Doctor Monroe is making the trip." The latter comment a convenient escape for Smith-Jones since the two had an understanding that the community always needed one of them on hand to deal with medical emergencies.

Truth be known, Smith-Jones was not a skilled automobile driver. His notoriety as an incompetent menace on the road was widely known. His only known match being the Prime Minister of Canada—who's driving mishaps were once described by Bob Edwards "… as another CPR wreck." Smith-Jones, probably was quite aware of his lack of skill, which would explain why he put so little mileage on the McLaughlin in the course of six years of ownership. Nick Thorpe, Carl Gassing's principle mechanic never failed to pronounce that it came into the shop—just like the day it was driven from the factory—each time it arrived for an annual spring tune up. Nick was also the only person, other than Smith-Jones, ever permitted to drive the auto, functioning as he did as paid chauffer, for those rare Sunday outings when Smith-Jones felt obliged to visit his wife's family. They lived some distance away, in a now forgotten town, somewhere between Coronation and Castor—a trip too far for Smith-Jones to handle. According to my father, Smith-Jones was terrified of highway driving even in a McLaughlin-Buick despite an automobile known for its power and outstanding road ability. Indeed, the cars became known as *Whisky Sixes* during the illegal whisky trade in an earlier and lively period of Alberta's history.

Moreover, when Smith-Jones did drive, he could not bring himself to drive the machine over twenty-five miles an hour. Because of this timidity on his part, Nick Thorpe was called upon to chauffeur. This time it would be with out compensation. Not that this ever entered into it as he was just happy to be going and long after Smith-Jones had left town, Thorpe was to confide, that on that trip he had the chance to put the auto through its paces with out the worry of the owner's nervous presence.

This latest bit of news put me in an adventurous mood and so I decided to celebrate a little by way of stopping off at Chang's on my way home. The object for going there was to try my luck at a winning a free pack of chewing gum. As it was a Saturday morning, my school-mate Johnny Chang was working behind the counter of the family establishment. I told him what I had learned and we fell enthusiastically into discussing the in and outs of the Tiger's forth coming trip to Edmonton. The conversation was brief because I had arrived almost at lunchtime and the place would soon fill with the regular noontime customers. Johnny's father was all business during those times and he usually asked a not unfriendly but brisk, "What you want boy?" as he was anxious to have the small boy, whoever he might be, dealt with and out of the way before the real business at hand commenced.

The deal for winning a free pack of gum was this: If there was a stick of black gum in the packet purchased, well ... they rewarded with one free pack. This sounds like a simple matter of chance except that there was a trick to dealing at Chang's. He dearly loved gambling and delighted in fooling his stream of young customers drawn to the Café to try their luck. Expecting to be winners, my gang almost never bought name brand chewing gum, knowing even, that it tasted better. Trouble with picking the right pack, was, simply put, the fact that Chang stacked the deck. Practical business, he thought of it. What he did was this; he gave himself better odds by mixing fresh cartons of gum with the old, in full knowledge that no lucky black sticks remained. In this way, he increased the odds against his clientele's chances of winning. Even so, the gum was cheaper than the established brands and as we fancied ourselves quite capable of outwitting Chang we bought our packs of gum from him. Accordingly, we developed strategies to try to beat him. Few of these actually worked because we based our strategies on extracting information out of Chang, who was a master at providing vague answers to probing questions. Furthermore, if pushed too hard for information, he simply turned away and walked back into the kitchen, secure in the knowledge the young customer was committed to buying. I asked Johnny if the black sticks were all gone. He shrugged casting his eyes to the heavens. It was enough. I knew none remained. I bought a pack anyway and didn't bother to open it up until after I had left the store.

13

During the night of Saturday February 24, the day before the big game, I awoke sometimes towards morning feeling cold. From the open bedroom door, I could see that the heater had burned to its lowest. Only a faint glow of burning embers was visible through the mica window of the heater door. The coldness of a low fire is not what awakened me, it was the sound of a towering wind shaking the very walls of our house and rattling the storm windows outside my room until it seemed they would implode right onto my bed. As well, I was certain the huge Manitoba maple standing close to my window must surely crash down upon the roof of our house. The sudden sound of one of its branches splitting away from the trunk reverberated like that of a rifle shot, fired upon a clear and frozen night. My parents, equally startled came anxiously into my room. Soon, the three of us were huddled together in the living room, peering out a frosted window and trying to determine how much damage had was inflicted upon the outside world.

The storm did not soon abate but continued to swirl snow and pack it upon the windowpanes. Visibility was such that we could see no further than the front gate. It was quite impossible, at this point, to tell what this rampaging late winter storm blasting through our community might be doing. The damage was caused by a fearsome, driving wind—later estimated to have reached velocities approaching fifty to sixty miles an hour gusting even higher—and the heavy wet snow, which was being driven into every crack and cranny of the house. In very short order, those windowpanes not actually covered with snow, frosted over. Snow began sifting under the rug, even though mother, the night before, had carefully placed it against the sill in an attempt to keep out any draft—father had not yet renewed the weather stripping. For now, once he had inspected the main parts of the house and tended to the stoves, Father determined that there was nothing else to be done and concluded that we might just as well all go back to bed and wait for morning. As a precaution, he declined to add any more wood to the fires reminding Mother and me of the tendency for the chimney to downdraft in extreme weather. It might not be safe to do anything just now, he said, and did promise to re-light the heater once daylight was upon us when we could more easily tend to it. Mother found an extra blanket and tucked it over my quilt. I lay there listening to the howl of the storm imagining that at any instant the roof might still blow off. I was quite certain that I could not possibly fall back to sleep and so was quite astonished to awaken in the full light of day. I heard too, a cheerful sound of a crackling wood fire and the welcoming smell of tea and toast coming from the kitchen. Arising from bed, I could see nothing through my frost-covered bedroom window until I scraped a tiny opening with a fingernail. The yard was now completely white, the air devoid entirely of wind sounds.

Once outside, we viewed a different world from that of the evening before. Telephone lines were down, small trees entirely bent to the ground, and ice-bound tree branches dangled from snow encrusted trunks. A rare sight seen as the result of the snowstorm itself had changed from snow to sleet and wet showers. This combination put a layer of frozen snowy ice upon every pole and tree within sight. Out in the back lane, the corner pole carrying both telephone and electrical power, had snapped and was hanging dangerously low to the ground. In the kitchen, mother was matter-of-factly making toast atop the wood-fired kitchen stove, utilizing a seldom-used wire grill. Our nickel-plated Westinghouse manual electric sat uselessly on the table along side a silent same brand five tube AM radio. These temporary material losses scarcely noticed so caught was I by the sudden brilliance of the morning sun.

Breakfast over, we took our leave of mother and set out on a journey over the snow-drifted streets. From what we could see, it was certainly going to take some time to restore power and telephone to Turnbull—many hours for certain, possibly into the next day, perhaps on into next week. We had no way of knowing how extensive the storm had been. Father, on the committee that would have to assess the situation, said we had best go down to Gassings' and find out what was what.

He decided against wearing his great coat knowing its length and bulk would be an encumbrance negotiating the deep, slushy snow, which had covered the streets all the way to the downtown. Sensibly, he pulled on a pair of six-buckle overshoes and chose to wear his weekend chore jacket—a common woollen pea jacket, a combination better suited to the conditions that had taken place. The effects of a bright, February morning, sun upon the fallen snow was causing slippery streets and water to drip off the roofs of buildings and houses all along our way. Consequently, we gave roofs a wide berth, particularly the faster melting east-facing ones. Even so, we occasionally got showered by small amounts of wet snow cascading off the opposite slopes. Even the mature Manitoba Maple trees lining our streets created a problem in that their branches, so heavily laden with snow, were often touching the sidewalks and creating barriers for walking pedestrians. The younger replacement trees, of more limber poplar and spruce, did not escape the elements either; many of them were bent from base to tip and lying flat to the ground. Yet, even with the warmth of the sun, it took several hours to melt away the weight of snow and ice.

Father did not even bother to check in at his Dental office once we reached the business section of town, reasoning that there was little likelihood of a patient in need of emergency treatment, his theory being that emergency patients always called at night and, by custom, he took no bookings for Saturday morning. Therefore, off we went directly to Carl Gassing's, as it was designated the team's starting point. Once inside, like everyone who had entered, we stopped to gawk at the seldom seen Smith-Jones' show room condition, McLaughlin-Buick. This we did, upon entering the garage, even before considering what the problems of the day might be.

Prior to our arrival, a number of team officials and some of the players were already discussing the problems. The big question: could the team even get out of Turnbull let alone make it as far as the main highway? Secondly, the question arose as to whether or not a full complement of players could be expected to show up and make a competitive team. If the Tigers were to default it was unlikely that another date could be set being that it was so late in the season. Several key players lived a few miles out of town and would undoubtedly have to come by team and sleigh providing the drifting hadn't made it too difficult even for horses. As to attempting the trip with an automobile, that was just out of the question.

"I think we will just have to wire the Edmonton Royals, say it is impossible and book another time," cautioned Smith-Jones, who was thinking about possible damage to his immaculate McLaughlin-Buick should it be driven over near impassable roads.

The Mayor, indecisive politician that he was, worked his way around the subject and wetted his finger to see which way the wind was blowing. He concluded, finally, that his position was much the same as Smith-Jones, and mistakenly thought it pretty close to that of Carl Gassing who had taken no position to this point but who was thinking upon the dilemma. The mayor looked hopefully at Carl. The immediate reaction to his first words was to laugh; all present thinking he was being quite droll. He was serious.

His suggestion was that they start out by clearing the road using Grandad Cade's wondrous home built wooden snowplough.

"Might work," said Doc.

"See here you're not serious. That old pile of scrap iron and boards hardly lasted two town blocks," the Mayor responded rather testily, thinking he was still being kidded about the last Cade episode.

"Not what you are thinking Alvin," put in Doc. "It wouldn't get us as far as the main road but might make a track across Chain Lakes and get us over to Mallard Beach which is but a half mile from the main road. Isn't that about what you had in mind, Carl?" Gassing having generated the idea only nodded agreement content for the moment to let the others work out some of the details.

"Maybe got something," agreed Charlie Sayer.

"If only we could get past that half-mile. Ice is certainly solid enough on the lake," mused my father, supportive of the idea.

"You really think that rickety old home-built can do the job?" Charlie Sayer turned the matter back to Carl Gassing.

"If we made up a convoy and had a few extra men with grain shovels, might just do it. Stick to the north shore and avoid any ice piles. Know anyone been out fishing lately?" asked Carl before turning it into a general question to the group.

Coach MacLean, who did know somebody, himself and Captain Jack, ice anglers both, picked up this idea immediately.

"Jack and me been out quite a bit lately. What I don't know, the icemaker does. I can tell you out on the lake most of that snow has blown into ridges leaving a lot of clear ice as the wind sweeps west to east. I think once we can get on to the lake itself we can very likely make Windy Point."

"Hold on boys!" said Charlie Sayer, thinking things out. "We can likely get as far as you say, but what about that half mile the other end of the lake? How we going to manage that? No team of horses is going to plough through the drifts on that stretch. Windy point didn't get its name for nothing."

"Right about that part," added Arch Macdonald whom no one, to this point, had asked about the necessary horsepower. "Team of horses can handle the two miles down the lake alright but as Charlie is saying, past Windy Point, those drifts will likely be belly deep ... horses are just not going to make it. Just a notion, but why not phone the Municipal Shop, get them to send out some heavy-duty equipment for that bad half mile? We'd pretty much be at the main road after that."

"Naw, road grader won't touch it," advised Carl Gassing, "Though somehow we get a Cat—referring to a D7 Caterpillar Tractor. County got a cat Alvin?"

"By George believe they have ... Get me on the phone and I'll find out for sure."

"Phone Lines are down. Talked with Miss Ellie before I came," Smith-Jones volunteered this latest bit of unwelcome news.

"Then that's out, boys," said the Mayor, "got to think of something else."

"Not much else we can do," concluded Carl Gassing speaking as much to himself as to the rest, while he was still thinking over the matter but coming up dry.

"Got an idea," said Norquist speaking out for the first time.

All eyes on the Creamery Man because he thinks things out before talking.

"That kid from Clear View? His old man is head of a Telephone Co-op."

"What kid Jalmer?" asked Carl Gassing.

"Plommer? Old man Plommer got his neighbours to put up a Barbwire Telephony service from just east of town over to Poplar Hill where they do a lot of their shopping. barbwire fences don't blow over much so might be we send a message over the Barbwire Telephony then relay the message from there over to the County Seat. Regular lines might be clear."

"Problem is if we do that then we got to contend with Mike Plommer, the old man himself. Had a bit of trouble with him at the game ..." Carl Gassing spoke, frowned and then paused as he recalled the earlier incident. "He's not likely to help us out ... told him we wouldn't be including his son in the line ups?"

"Hell put him back," Charlie Sayer spoke up getting right to the pith of the matter.

"What about it coach?"

All eyes turned to coach MacLean.

"Well I did kinda leave it open. Didn't say yes exactly and not a firm no."

"That's not like you to leave the decision up in the air like that," said Carl Gassing knowing MacLean all too well so figured there must be an angle.

"Oh pretty simple we've got three of our boys down with bad cases of the gripe. Doc Monroe doesn't know how quickly they might recover so it wasn't much of a decision to leave young Plommer on the ready list. Wouldn't hurt to bring him along in case someone gets hurt or our boys on the sick list don't recover in time. Fact is we won't know till game time even if we get there."

"Well, if you can stomach Mike Plommer we could try that route," the Mayor added.

"Not big decisions then I guess. Just how are we going to get you as far as Plommer's, Alvin?" Gassing was sizing up the Mayor's pot bellied physique and a sedentary body that clearly said no to any heroic tramp through the snows.

"Well I know I am not going to walk," said the Mayor quite emphatically.

"No, don't expect you to do that. Could we send a younger man with your request?" asked Carl Gassing, still the most vocal of the group.

"Good idea as long as Alvin puts together the message it won't matter who we send it with; even a couple of the lads out on skis would do," my father offered.

"Might work," speculated Charlie Sayer. "Look, if it's all right with you, how be it we send that lad of yours along with maybe that young Blair boy … friend of his isn't he? They are both reliable I hear. Send them out on their skis."

"I think that would be all right if Jamie is willing to do it," replied my father for me as I was nodding my head in agreement.

"Agreed?" Charlie asked the question.

There was a further nodding of heads all around including my father. That is how we came to be like the ancient Greek couriers bearing messages. Not exactly, Marie Chapdelaine, Laura Secord or the American, Paul ... "what's his name", as the irreverent Newfies would put it, but important and exciting nevertheless. The journey was made even more interesting knowing that we would have to deal with blunt-mannered Plommer, a rough sort of man rumoured to be ever ready to chase unwelcome "guests" off his property with a loaded shotgun. True or not we believed it and the two of us stayed quite clear of any known Plommer fence lines whenever we had ventured into the hilly terrain of that part of the County in search of hares.

As expected, Plommer wasn't exactly all smiles when we skied up his driveway nor were his pair of mongrel farm dogs who thought to sample us for lunch. I had nervously prepared myself for just such an encounter, counselling Blair to not look. Don't look that kind of dog square in the eye but just stand still, let them smell around you till they think you're no threat. Do it even if you're scared and remember to talk to them a little, which was practically word for word from what I had learned from my Uncle Hart. It was good to have a plan of battle, as it were, but plans like battles are never a sure thing. The pair of wolf like beasts did not bark, as most dogs will; instead, they circled stiff legged about, watching for our slightest advance.

"Just don't move and they won't bite," I spoke it aloud less as a reminder of strategy than as a sudden and urgent need to speak out bravely in the dark.

Still Uncle's advice was taken and all went well. Yet, remembering that first occasion still can send shivers up my spine whenever I conjure up an image of those snarling beasts.

Fortunately, our ordeal was short-lived, ending when Plommer's son Mike came to our rescue and called the beasts off. Afterwards, they didn't even bother a look, for which we were grateful.

Old man Plommer was not at all apologetic. "Them dogs ain't never going to bother long's you keep your distance and ain't up to no good."

"Yes sir."

"You didn't come out all the way out here just to visit. Must be somethin' important you got. Your daddy sent you?" He directed the question at me knowing whose son I was and not quite placing Blair.

"Yes sir he did, but it's a message from the Mayor and the hockey club. Mr. Norquist said you would help," I blurted without any thought of clarification as to what the matter was about. "Here it is," I handed him an envelope.

"Know what it says boy?" he inquired balancing the envelope in his hand as one would when weighing out a sample of grain. He seemed in no particular hurry to open it and asked once more whether I knew what information might be in it. Although, in fact, I did know the gist of the matter, I certainly had not read the note itself; but, he was persistent and so I offered up an edited version of the situation, as I knew it.

"That a fact."

"I think so. That's what I was told," I added, backing down a little, just in case the letter did not contain a reference to his son Mike making the team roster.

"Well you better come on inside while we figure what we're going to do." With that he turned on his heel and took the few steps back inside. We stashed our skis at the door and then stepped inside with Mike following in last. We shed our jackets and boots at the door and took a place on a bench at the kitchen table. Mr. Plommer sat himself down in one of two bow back chairs. A brisk fire was burning in the kitchen range and Mrs. Plommer busied about her work, but not pausing to acknowledge us, not even when old man Plommer spoke to her.

"Set two more places, these here boys going to join us. You like stew don't you? Might as well that's what you are going to get, stew and biscuits. The Missus, here makes the best biscuits and stew in the county." This caused a faint smile to pass over Mrs. Plommer's passive face but it was her only response.

"Yes sir." We waited respectfully wondering why he had not yet opened the envelope. Finally, after a rambling discourse on stew and biscuits, he opened the envelope, a rather official looking brown envelope bearing an Insurance Company letter head, unfolded the letter, holding it first upside down at arms length, then finally handed it to his son Mike.

"Here boy read it out for me. I don't rightly know where I put my spectacles," he said and with out comment the son then turned the letter right side up and read it aloud "Read that part again where it says you are in the line-up."

"Of course if we get the co-operation from the county we will expect your boy Mike to be at Gassing's Garage and Livery promptly at eight o'clock Saturday morning ready for departure ... also he is responsible for a few personal supplies as listed below."

"He don't say what line your on do it?" questioned Plommer brow furrowing as he spoke being forever suspicious of glad tidings.

"Up to the coach Pa, Mr. McKenzie don't ever say until game time."

"He don't huh?"

"No."

"Well I guess it means what it says. Damn well better, I can tell you. Well maw, put on the stew, it's time to eat," he instructed and Mrs. Plommer without a word proceeded to serve the two men and ourselves. She did not take a place at the table the entire time we were there.

The stew, as good as the billing, demanded seconds but Blair and I were too polite to ask. Plommer, more observant than we had expected, looked at our cleaned up plates, looked over at his wife and indicated a second serving.

"Just a small amount," I said. "Its awfully good Mrs. Plommer," I added getting a smile a slight nodding of the head and a soft "umm". I didn't think I would like the lamb because Uncle always made a face whenever it was mentioned. He got too much of it in the Great War. "Mutton," so he said, "was just one of the hardships of war." Despite Uncle's opinion, Mrs. Plommer's stew was just awfully good.

"I didn't know you raised sheep Mr. Plommer," I added innocently, bringing much laughter from Plommer, his son, and even a
tight little smile from Mrs. Plommer.

"Yes. Well, I don't right at the moment," he responded as soon as
he could contain his merriment. It was not until some time later did I
learn that we had been eating venison.

Uncle said that it was a well-known fact that many Clear Sky district farmers regularly poached deer. It was more an economic necessity than any desire to elude the game laws. Clear Sky, it seemed, was
best noted for bush, rough hills, ponds and sloughs. Not the best
place in the world to try to farm, he had explained, adding that's why
you saw mostly range cattle and horses being raised there; with mostly
the small meadows located around sloughs used as the primary source
of hay in the district. People living in Clear Sky District tended to be
a little hard bitten, which explained why the dozen or so farmers living in the district refused to give up their barbwire telephone service.
This despite areas like Turnbull being served by one of a growing
number of Mutual Companies linked to AGT switching systems; the
Government still deeming itself too poor to finance a single province-
wide telephone service and neither Bell Telephones nor any other
commercial firm was willing to do it for them.

Plommer, coming up from Oregon State, had experience with
Barbwire Telephony and subsequently convinced his neighbours to
team up and construct one of their own. Considering that on these
short line systems, you needed little equipment other than a number
of connected hand cranked and battery operated telephones to make
it work, it was a far cheaper network than that supplied by the Companies. Doc, who knew about such things, explained that besides
being simple and cheap to operate; the secret to it lay in making good
ground contact at each home station and Clear Sky, apparently
because of a high water table, had pretty much ideal conditions. The
down side seemed to be in keeping the actual barbwire carrier lines
from grounding out. Consequently, the rural party line co-op was

dependent upon how conscientious the membership was in inspecting and repairing lines.

I was curious enough about the system to ask Plommer about it while I was there. The man, quite eloquent in his own way, promptly launched into a description of its workings. After a rudimentary explanation, he got down to the problems. They were it seemed few. Mostly, he said, the telephone system shut down because some damned old cow pushed through a fence snapping a wire and breaking connections. As well, during particularly wet or sometimes snowy weather, a clump of tall wet grass or a drifted pile of heavy snow would lie against the wires and ground them out. No, he didn't think that would be the case this time. There just hadn't been much of a snowfall out his way, which, of course, was the hope of the Hockey Committee in sending the two of us east to Clear View. As suspected, the district had indeed escaped the wrath of the storm that dumped upon Turnbull. In fact, I learned later, areas northeast of Turnbull also escaped the heavy fall. We had seen that this was so the farther we skied east of town to the Plommer place. Later in life, a climatologist once showed me a map of the Wind Roses of Alberta confirming the capricious nature of our weather and allowing for in the area in which one lives to experience a snow storm when there is nary a cloud in the sky somewhere else. And, it was because this capricious nature of Alberta weather that the Tigers' management felt it worth trying to dig the way from Turnbull to the main highway some twenty miles away, part of which would be a twelve-mile stretch of lake ice.

"Travel a hundred miles, travel through three weather systems," was Captain Jack's oft stated opinion. His remarks gave way to cautious optimism that this would be the case on that day back in the spring of 1939 when the attempt was made. The trick for the Turnbull Tigers was going to be in finding a way to get from one road system to another.

Plommer, unable to resist the chance of his son playing in the big game, enthusiastically lent his support but only after he had the contents of the message read to him several times. He asked over again about parts that did not seem to have specificity. Finally convinced his son would indeed be on the roster, he made his way over to the telephone and cranked it fiercely until he got through to the required destination. He was equally vigorous in shouting the message into the mouthpiece of the telephone itself, thinking it only logical that the very power of his voice would carry over long-distance to the County Shops; even if, in fact, his conversation was only going to get him as far as the Poplar Hill General store where the line terminated. It was then necessary to have the proprietor, Albert Marshall, contact the County Shops over the regular telephone system. The marvel of it all was that Plommer, unable to read, had the message clearly in his mind and quite articulately explained it all back to Marshall. Eventually word got through to the County Foreman, who once clear as to what was being requested, confirmed that the County did have a D7 and said he would personally get it fired up ready to go while awaiting the necessary authorization to send it out.

We left as Plommer and Marshall worked out the details of the next call to the County Reeve who had the authority to send out the Cat. Plommer assured us, as we left that the task was as good as done and that once he relayed the Turnbull Tigers plan of action back to the County Foreman, he would send son Mike to town with the go ahead, at which time the Caravan crossing the lake could then proceed—his son included.

14

A good crowd of more than twenty people had already gathered by the time we arrived. While predominantly men and boys, there was also an exuberant cheering section of young women from the Ladies Broom Ball Club who had boy friends, brothers or husbands on the team. Quite a few came even after we did: several local farm families, having driven in and out for the fun, a small group of men regularly seen gathered somewhere downtown, and some teen-age girls arrived, in part, because they anticipated an equivalent group of teen-aged boys to also be there to see and be seen. The outdoor broadcast most certainly had provided an acceptable and exceptional reason for meeting and mingling as of a Sunday afternoon.

Doc Rafferty, despite being a club official, chose not go to Edmonton, devoting, instead, his energies in helping to conceive this unique game-simulation for the benefit of the local Turnbull citizens. It was one of his last civic ventures and perhaps the most enterprising; failing health caught up to him during wartime. He suffered from acute diabetes which eventually forced him to hospital, from which he never came back. Different than most even in death, his funeral instructions included a disposition for his remains to be cremated—an unheard of practise in Turnbull. Father said afterwards that Doc Rafferty, once having a posting with the East India Company, likely got the idea from there.

Arch McDonald and several other equally civic-minded fans, revelling in the novelty of the proceedings, lent a hand at setting things up. Arch had pulled his dray in front of Doc's shop, where the two of them were now attaching a makeshift set of steps on to the dray's back end giving easier access to the make shift stage. Charlie Sayer, there to do the play by play, rounded out the crew.

The place looked a lot like our Dominion Day and October Fest days. Doc had a splendid banner strung right across the false front of his little shop announcing, *"TIGERS PLAYOFF GAME LIVE,"* and with it went an elaborate game board for mounting on the front boards of the dray. A lectern and accountant's stool were added a few steps up front of the board as well as a megaphone, borrowed from Auten's Auctioneering, sitting handily by. Still the game board, the most visible thing on stage, was what immediately caught the eye. Doc had painted stylized versions of hockey players, with all their paraphernalia as embellishments to the board's perimeter, much in the style of the theatre drop screens of the day, and lacking only the customary advertisements of local merchants. I still remember our town's only rolled theatre screen, beset with classical figures and a gauze-draped nude drawn and painted by Doc Rafferty who claimed it was merely a copy of some great work of art thereby deflecting criticism from the more prudish townsfolk. I remember being fascinated by the painted lady myself and trying to look nonchalant while staring up at her charms. The occasions for viewing taking place only during local theatrical performances or times when I could afford a Saturday afternoon movie—the roll down curtain having a mid-section painted white, doubling also as the projection screen. Such decorative aspects aside—There was no nude on the sports board—Doc took a very draftsmen like approach to it with separate boxes drawn in to display the names of the individual players, coaches, the team officials as well as a movable board to show the periods. The other drawn areas he designated for the recording of scores, penalties, time, game officials and the like. Even Smith-Jones, not overly taken to much public display cried, "Good show!" when he saw it. My father's comment was that, "... old Doc had certainly outdone himself this time." I think every one there shared that opinion.

And there were others helping to make the final game an event to remember.

Lee Chang and his son Johnny had set up an outdoor kitchen in front of his restaurant and the two of them were already busy serving up hot chocolate, tea, coffee and fresh donuts contributed by Swenson's Bakery; cream and milk supplied by Turnbull Cream and Butter—Norquist, the owner, also owning the local Dairy.

It didn't take long for the two of us to succumb to Lee Chang's urging and check out the serving. Son Johnny just grinned and let his father do the talking.

"Come over here, I got good stuff. Chocolate, nice tea, coffee … come on boy what you want?" Chang pitched and I, not having brought any pocket money, stammered out my inability to pay. "Never mind money boy. You father got plenty. Here George," he urged, familiarly using my father's given name. "Buy these boys hot drink and donut. All going to the hockey team. Fifty cents maybe more …" Father did buy for both Blair and myself while Chang good naturedly cajoled my father to put in lots of money. His son Johnny served up the donuts and was cheerful like his father if, perhaps a little less exuberant, still, I had the impression, whenever we went to their restaurant that he would rather be doing something else somewhere else. His favourite pursuits were playing hockey, like the rest of us, or just curling up with a favourite book.

Once we had our fill of hot chocolate and donuts, we did some looking about ourselves; essentially looking to see who, besides ourselves, were in attendance. Surprising us just a bit was the presence of Smith-Jones himself. I suppose considering he had lent his beloved McLaughlin-Buick to help the team make the trip to Edmonton we need not have been. Moreover, he was in a jocular mood acknowledging both Blair and myself even before greeting my father. We were a bit mystified at the attention, still remembering our last encounter at the magazine rack in his Drugstore.

"I say George," he addressed my Father, "I've been told by Jack Rafferty that he expects to be able to relay scores from the telegraph office right to here in a matter of only five seconds once the message has been received. What do you think about that?"

"I'd say we are in for a very good show. Better than direct over radio. With this good crowd out here to cheer our lads on, it should be second only to being there. Did Doc say how this whole thing is going to work?"

"It starts first with our man on a local telephone line at the arena in Edmonton. Jack gained access to a press box with a local phone line. And from there ... Turk McKenzie knows someone with the Edmonton Bulletin ... the press box will not be using it as the Bulletin reporter will not be in attendance. This was not a semi-pro game or a champion series of wide importance to the Bulletin readers."

"Well I think we ought to have a word with the Bulletin about that," responded Father sounding a trifle indignant."

"Right you are George."

At this point in the conversation, I got to ask a few questions of my own. The big one being the question of why didn't our man just phone the play-by-plays direct to Turnbull?

Smith-Jones and Father both jumped in with the explanation that money was at the root of it, the club not having any readily available cash money to cover the cost of a long distance phone line. The Bulletin's phone came free and so did the Telegraph line courtesy CN Telegraph which had been arranged by an ex-Turnbull operator largely because there would be little or no commercial traffic at that time and if need arose for any emergency transmissions, of course those messages would take precedent. The line was open at all times anyways, so it was only a matter of having an operator at either end: our local operator and the ex-Turnbull operator at Edmonton both allowing to the effect that it was just something to do.

"Jolly good of them both," said Smith-Jones, expressing just about the view of everyone there. Dave Fisher's father did the local relaying from the station to Rafferty's, the Turnbull phone office agreeing to keep one line open just to carry the game results. It being a Sunday afternoon, few calls were expected. It sounded complicated and exciting.

And the last link was Charlie Sayer doing play-by-play. He was a good talker and always had a store of anecdotes to use for all occasions. We knew he wouldn't let us down on that score. So with head set on and microphone in hand, Charlie was all set to take the first batch of messages. Saying he was ready to announce the play-by-play.

Voices, from the crowd started hollering back. "She's loud and clear," cried a male voice.

"Man's a genius," from another.

"Hurrah for old Doc Rafferty!" followed by loud clapping and cheering.

Charlie with everything ready launched into his play by play: "You folks hear what the Edmonton Goaler had to say about our little rink here in town? No. Well I'll tell you. Get this ... he told me the first game right here in Turnbull was just like playing water polo. The best swimmers on ice were the winners ... ha ha. Rich isn't it?"

Charlie continued to chat up the crowd as everyone got into the spirit of things.

"Here is a late bulletin ... Coach McKenzie sends word through his wife that our three boys with nose colds: Jameson, Bo Beales and Whizzer Jackson, are pretty much over it. Course my supplying a good bottle of Seagram's undoubtedly did some good. Ha, ha. Doctor Monroe didn't have much other to offer ... wait eight days he says. Of course the boys didn't have eight days to wait."

"Glad to hear they are in shape," my father added.

There was more cheering then ... "Here it is folks brought direct from the Edmonton South Side Arena. Here it is," he repeated, "listen carefully." He paused dramatically, "A message from Coach McKenzie: I feel it is a safe bet that we can take the cup and bring it back to Turnbull." The crowd erupted into more cheering and applause. "Now here are the line-ups. For Edmonton: first line Duchak-Captain, Clapton, and Mayther; second line Cornish, Boucher, and Bell, with Cameron the floater; defense—another dramatic pause—on defense Lorenz, Bouten and Jardine, and, almost forgot, that classy young third string and the equally classy goaler, Kuzmac, who is again in front of the nets. And I...."

Once the Tiger's names had been read out, there followed a prolonged cheering and clapping, with a few "Go Tigers Go!" thrown in for good measure.

At the air break, I got a chance to sort out a puzzler. Why, I wanted to know, did we have more players dressed than did Edmonton? To my surprise, Smith-Jones had the answer. Both teams were allowed the same number and only the Tigers had added two more because they were worried about the incidents of fevers and colds amongst the team's players so they listed the entire roster. Then too, coach McKenzie wanted a couple of the younger players suited just to give them the feel for higher calibre play even if they didn't get any ice time—unlikely unless the game got very lop sided one way or the other.

"Play-by-play coming right up," Charlie announced upon receiving his first set of relayed messages. Looking intently at the copy as if committing it to memory, he finally took a deep breath and began. "Edmonton wins the draw, Cornish has it ... down the ice and is knocked down ... a hard check by Busher MacLean, over to Tucker Monroe, checked by Boucher, Edmonton still in possession. Over to Bell, Jackson steps on and intercepts, Jackson going down over to ... stolen by Duchak a break one man back Duchak sailing in over the line passes to Clapton. Shoots ... missed the net! Tigers' goaler Sid Simpson takes the rebound off the boards and pushes it ahead to Bo Beales-come on Ti-gerrs!"

There followed a break in play-by-play giving the hometowners time to talk amongst themselves. The delay, although not long, was caused by Arch having to hop on and off the dray in order to collect each sheet sent over by the CNR operator. For all the planning, no one, Doc included, had anticipated this might be a problem. Blair and I volunteered our help. Blair scrambled up on the dray and I ducked under to the front of the box almost tripping over the *eveners* in the process. A couple other boys also vied for the job but Blair and

I, clearly the front-runners, got the job. I worked the inside beside Doc, running the messages to Blair who waited outside the door, before relaying them up to Arch who stood waiting on top the dray. It was like a paper bucket brigade differing in that we were trying to fire up the crowd rather than dampen it down.

The message chain sorted out, Charlie resumed his game description. "A Tigers rush, and Beales passes to Jimmy Brody, Brody a shot dead on," he paused dramatically before continuing and the crowd held its breath awaiting the moment to cheer, not knowing the outcome. Then collectively they "oohed" their voices in disappointment. Hardly pausing to take a breath, he continued.

"Kuzmac robs Brody. A hot one folks but a save by Kuzmac. Taken by Royals … it's that flashy third line out now making a play … Tigers backing up waiting for that patented shoot and run. There is the shot … Shultz holds the winger back, Big Plume retrieves for the Tigers, a quick pass out … stolen by Cameron who shoots it back in. Big Plume races into the corner, gets it. Again a pass out to Cameron … a shot on goal! Simpson stops that one." A collective sigh of relief heard coming from the crowd.

"Busher MacLean grabs the rebound, starts a rush to the Royals end with both teams changing on the go. Busher up to Tucker Monroe … a break for Monroe. He beats his man and is going in alone, tries to split the defense and is taken out by Lorenz and Bouten. Now Duchak starts a rush … doesn't get far as Bo Beales hooks the puck away and leads a rush back to the Edmonton end. He passes off to Jackson over to Brody and … a weak shot … hits a defenseman and … something missing here. I don't know what happened folks. It's a goal for Edmonton? Doesn't make sense. Hold off on putting up a score Arch."

Doc Rafferty, looking as puzzled as Charlie, got right on the phone to Miss Elsie and asked for an immediate connection through to the CN Operator. Connections made, listened to the explanation, and then uttered a terse, "Sorry for the interrupt, explain later, but here I've also got a new message."

We moved that one fast, me to Blair, to Arch, to Charlie all quick as a wink. Charlie momentarily studied the written messages hoping for a Tigers' reprieve and ruefully explained, "We should have got it. Our boys were way ahead on the play."

"Bad break. Now we'll have to play it wide open," said Father, expressing the view of most of the fans.

"Can't do it," said Smith-Jones. "Ice sheets too big. Our team is not used to big ice."

Although several local fans had speculated that this might happen, only now did the full implications of the Tigers performing on a big ice surface hit home. The first score of the game, by Edmonton, set some beginning of doubt creeping into the minds of even some of the most avid fans.

Charlie carried on, "Face-off, it's Tigers. Grabbed by Jackson, Bo Beales slaps a hot one right on Kuzmac's pads. Joe Schmall right in there to take the rebound. Loses it and he is down. Joe Schmall is down. Hit over the head by Lorenz. Schmall is hurt. Referee Ross blows the whistle. There is going to be a penalty!" This news set up an immediate chorus of boos and encouraging shouts by the gathered fans.

"I don't believe this," Charlie although back into his impartial announcer's mode could not hide his disbelief. "Arch check and see if I got the message right. Says here, Dutch Jamieson gets the penalty. Lorenz hits Schmall over the head and Dutch gets a penalty!" The fans shouts of protest ran through out the site. My mother, said later, that she could hear the crowd roar every time there was something important happening but could never tell if was good or bad.

Smith-Jones, quite agitated because of this turn of events, summed up pretty much what the crowd was thinking. "By George," he shouted out and waving his fast emptying flask for emphasis, "we should never have agreed to that *B-league* referee from Edmonton." He continued his wild waving of the flask to a point where father had to remind him politely about being in a public place. Smith-Jones, apologizing for the indiscretion, headed the flask back to the folds of his Buffalo coat while pausing, momentarily, to offer my father a pull. Father declined, but I think, although I never saw him do it, he had partaken of a fair amount of Smith-Jones flask by this time.

Charlie ... "The fans are booing. Get this; the Edmonton fans are booing the referee after that call on Dutch Jamison. Play resumes. Tigers short handed for the next two minutes. Edmonton has it ... loose puck. Dave Fisher now playing on the penalty killing passes over to Leon Shultz who rushes over the line ... a shot! Another save by Kuzmac. Now Bouten ... no ... Edmonton defenseman trips Shultz as he re-positions and this time Edmonton takes a penalty.... Both teams even numbers now. Lorenz takes the puck, slashes Tucker Monroe who is back out on the even strength. No penalty ... Busher MacLean steps in, knocking down Lorenz, takes away the puck. A rush on the Edmonton net!" The Turnbull fans once again erupted into loud cheering and whistling.

Charlie, in an off-mike aside to Arch, asked for the next message; then back to his mike, "Sorry folks have to wait for the next message."

He took a break from his reporting and having worked up quite a sweat by this time he took the opportunity to retrieve his water jug that was laying on a straw bundle. The bundle itself propped up there to support the scoreboard. The board itself clearly showed the telling results from the first period: Royals 1, Tigers 0. Doc Rafferty's splendid score board was indeed doing the job properly but his craftsmanship, while much admired, did little to soften the blow of our team's failure to score.

The next message in Doc Rafferty's hastily written but highly legible script, passed quickly from me to Blair, to Arch, then on up to Charlie..

"Here it is folks. A penalty! Tucker Monroe gets a penalty but it was Lorenz once again doing the dirty work. Referee Ross is standing off to the side thinking it over. Some difficulty getting Tucker to go into the box. He stands by his decision, Tigers get another penalty and this Edmonton crowd is once again booing the Referee."

"I should hope so; anyone can see what's going on." Smith-Jones opined, his voice now uncharacteristically loud. Father, whose voice was also becoming elevated, pointed out that none of us here could, in fact, see any of the game at all. This observation by my father resulted in much laughter by Smith-Jones and himself. The humour of which quite escaped Blair and me.

"Quite so, George, quite so." Smith-Jones finally managed to speak after a brief spell of throaty laughter and several tugs upon his moustache, "What I mean to say is that the refereeing seems a bit partial. Don't you think? What do you think young James?" Then, in an aside to my father, added, "Important to get the young peoples opinion on matters such as these eh? Quite."

My opinion? I was too taken aback to have any at all. This the same person, who mere days before, casting himself in the role of keeper of young boys morals, had turfed us out of his Drugstore because he found us exploring the racier section of the magazine stand? Still, I must confess, I had gotten to almost liking Smith-Jones by this time; and it was not merely because of the hot chocolate and cookies. It was, I think, rather a developing perspective on the sometimes mystifying behaviour of adults. Next, also because of the flask and, perhaps, just for the fact that before the game was ended, he took to calling me Jamie in a friendly if not affectionate tone. Between periods, having gotten quite bottle mellow he insisted on sending Blair and me back to Chang's for each to have another cup of hot cocoa and donut. I protested mildly until father gave his nod of approval thus sending the two of us happily off to enjoy our unexpected good fortune. In later years, upon recalling Smith-Jones' behaviour, my father told me that one of Smith-Jones' great disappointments in life was not having had any children; something to do with Mrs. Smith-Jones, my father thought but did not know for certain; as it was almost always assumed, in those days, that the fault lay with the woman. Although Smith-Jones never admitted to it, he had a great fondness for youth and boys. It seemed to be part of his nature to hide his emotions in this way. His exterior manner likely resulted from his English upbringing.

The first period ended much as it had started. The play a bit ragged with Tigers having two men in the penalty box for rough play and more booing from a near partisan Edmonton crowd. Even my father, the most temperate of men, was agreeing that the calls did seem a bit one sided. I had never heard him say anything like that before. Although he did equivocate somewhat by saying that Kuzmac was having a very fine game, adding patriotically that Sid Simpson could hardly be faulted for the one goal allowed during several minutes of very uneven play by our boys.

The period ended with no additional scoring. Tigers still short a man. "If we can just hold out on those penalties our boys can get down to business and win this game," said Charlie Sayer, summarizing the play that marked the end of the first period.

During intermission, Charlie Sayer decided to do the play-by-play using a delayed start in order to enable the Broadcast Team to keep ahead of the play. I think it was mainly Doc's idea, but the team members each had a hand in deciding, ourselves included. The thinking was that by making these few changes, some of the first-period breakdowns would be avoided. It was further agreed to keep each of the team members at their same posts. The new arrangement suited me just fine because I would be able to get information ahead of the crowd as well as continue to catch some of Charlie's innovative game descriptions. In fact, things went so smoothly in the second and third that more than one citizen thought it should became a regular part of away-from-home league finals.

"Play about to start," called out Arch Macdonald, getting back the crowds attention while Charlie Sayer organized his sheets.

Charlie, having gotten a second wind, launched into the second period. "Both teams now on the ice ... oh oh change of line-ups for the Tigers. Tucker Monroe out penalty killing with Leon Shultz and Busher MacLean. Whizzer Jackson the floater looking for a break away. Edmonton takes the face-off makes a nice rush shoves off Cornish with a nice clean check and … What is going on? Tucker Monroe gets a penalty. Tigers now short a third man for 10 seconds and yes folks," he paused dramatically, "Edmonton crowd again booing the referee. Edmonton up ice … here's Duchak … a wicked shot right on. Simpson gloves it, forces another face-off. Dutch Jamieson about to come on … Whizzer takes the face-off, grabs the puck, retreats behind his own net, fakes a pass then whips it just over the blue line taken quickly by Dutch Jamieson. Going end to end a brilliant play oh … forced into the corner. Those Edmonton defensemen are fast folks especially on the big ice. Play again getting quite ragged just twenty seconds before Monroe is back on … the teams are again at even strength, Jackson goes off, the crowd giving him a well-deserved hand. Maurice Francour taking his place. Over to Shultz … back to Jimmy Brody who has replaced Jamieson, Dave Fisher on for Busher … Fisher hasn't seen much action. Good solid player doesn't quite have the legs to go against this young fast Royals team—Charlie musing and adding more colour bits than play-by-play at this point—the Tigers just slowing down the play and keeping possession till they can get back to strength. Monroe back on the ice … a quick break over the Edmonton line by Monroe slashed by Lorenz. Lorenz doing a lot of slashing in this game. Again no penalty. The Edmonton crowd again boos the referee for not catching that one. Whizzer Jackson back on comes right in and again the Edmonton goalie is tested. Whizzer is dumped after he made the play. A lot of rough stuff going on here."

At this turn of events, the Turnbull fans took to loud booing, some even shaking their fists in the air at the offending officials so caught up were they in the perceived reality of Charlie's simulcast.

Charlie, looking pleased with his delivery, continued on, "Lorenz in against Monroe and butt-ends Monroe with his stick … there is going to be a penalty … got to wait for the next sheet to see who is going to get it. Ah, damn. What is this? Penalty to Monroe. Referee is standing off to the side thinking it over. He stands by the decision. Tiger player gets a penalty and the crowd is booing again. I can just see a shaking of heads amongst the crowd no one has ever heard the likes of. A lot of rough play. Royals seemed to be taking liberties and getting way with it."

The second period, as play went on, and as Charlie Sayer was to described it after the broadcast, "Was all raggedy assed." The scores remained the same, one goal for them and none for us.

The third period hardly got going before another incident occurred. Lorenz came out of his own zone and got decked with an absolutely clean check by big and rugged George Big Plume who had played little, sent out by Turk McKenzie in hopes his presence might change the character of the game and slow the fast skating Royals down. Maurice Francour centered the line with Barney Plummer on left wing. Our best men now out on defense, Leon Shultz and Busher MacLean, our biggest men, together forming a formidable defensive line. The same strategy with a slightly different cast had tied up the first game. From Charlie, "the last line change sent out Duchak, Clapton and Mayer on the forward line, and Lorenz and Bouten on defense—certainly Edmonton's most effective line. Turk figured just to wear the Edmonton line down; taking a chance that by doing so, he might allow a lesser Royals line a chance to run away with the period. As insurance against that happening, he put the Whizzer Jackson line opposite Edmonton's number two line and then shifted the Tucker Monroe line to face the extremely fast but less experienced Edmonton third line.

"Smart move. Might backfire," shouted out a crowd pessimist.

"We were not winning so we had to try something." Coach McKenzie was later quoted as saying, in the Turnbull Record

Suddenly from Charlie, "Late flash in folks, they have put Lorenz off. Coach or referee—we don't know why but Lorenz is out of the game. Referee must have had a change of heart. Hold on folks." The urgency in his voice brought the level of talk down to a whisper. The crowd waited. "Not good news. Lorenz is hurt and they have had to take him to the hospital. Our boys are going to feel bad about that I can tell you. I think I speak for all present in voicing the opinion that we don't want no hospital injuries. We just want to beat them.

There was general agreement from the Turnbull fans at this revelation.

"Sorry to hear that," my father said, speaking to Smith-Jones who had now switched over to Chang's coffee, as he was feeling tipsy and his speech had become muted. "Didn't much like the way Lorenz was doing things but from what we saw here in town he is a pretty classy player and we've no wish to beat them with injuries."

"Right you are George," echoed Smith-Jones, beginning to feel stabilized after drinking a second draught of coffee. Then added, "Would not be at all sporting."

Charlie, hardly pausing, continued, "While there is a stop in the play let's just take a moment to thank Doc Rafferty for this great set up and for all he has done to bring us the game. Arch, get Rafferty out here so's we can show him our appreciation...." Doc Rafferty, not comfortable in personal limelight, made a perfunctory appearance at the door of his shop and acknowledged the three cheers hollered out by the gathered citizens. Charlie went on to also acknowledge the volunteer telegraph operators, telephone staff, Arch Macdonald—even put in a word for Blair and me—the food crews from Chang's and Swenson's Bake Shop." He then thanked the entire gathering before resuming his play-by-play description.

"Here we are again folks right near the end of the third period direct to you courtesy the CN and Miss Elsie down at the Telephone office and, of course the fine showing here today of our own Doc Rafferty. The game is still tied one to nothing. Oh, what's this? Thanks Arch." A few unintelligible words were spoken between Charlie and Arch before Charlie was back-on-mike. "There is a stoppage in play. Team Manager Carl Gassing is talking to referee Ross. Must be something about the rules would be my guess. Team managers don't usually have words with the referee during games. Just wait a second till we get the next bulletin. Hope you have all enjoyed the afternoon. Shows great community spirit. I'm going to say just that in my next editorial. Okay here it is … team manager Gassing is protesting Edmonton Royals for packing the blue line. It's against conference rules. He has asked for a penalty to be assessed against Edmonton. The rules say no more than three players can be packed behind the blue line. Royals have stuck the whole darn team behind the line for the last five minutes of the game in an effort to shutout Turnbull. It's to no avail. No penalty to Edmonton."

Once again, the locals indulged in much booing and catcalling.

"Play resumes … the Royals still have every man behind the line. The Crowd has gotten into this and there is now constant booing from the fans as the game winds down. Whizzer Jackson gets the puck, shoots into the corner and Tucker Monroe charges in after it … Got all our big men but for Whizzer on for the last few moments. Oh, oh, Monroe digs it out carries in behind the net, Bouten and Jardine after him. He flips it back over to Busher MacLean … Duchak after him … MacLean flips a pass over Duchak's stick and Whizzer Jackson swoops in and gets a clean shot away … right on … Kuzmac makes the save. The amazing Mr. Kuzmac robs us again … rebound … Kuzmac stops Dutch Jamieson's wrist shot and Bouten grabs the puck, over to Duchak … the Royals are breaking out over the line … coming on fast only one man back … Leon Shultz is the only man back … Clapton and Sid Simpson coming out challenging the shooter, Clapton passes back to Bouten shoots from the blue line.… scores'"

There was a still in the crowd. No one present was prepared for an ending like this. After a few moments, Charlie spoke up.

"Well folks that was one helluva game. Didn't quite end the way we expected but you know those boys of ours did us proud." There followed murmurs of agreement as we shut down for the night and started heading home while Charlie finished off with thanks to the CNR Telegraph, Miss Elsie at the telephone office, Chang's and the rest of the participants.

"Quite agree. Quite agree!" Said Smith-Jones and neither my father nor I could think of anything further to say.

Epilogue

I don't often see many of my boyhood friends and companions, nor do I travel back to Turnbull with any regularity, although I try to arrange time for an occasional visit during Summer Fair days. The last time, I met up with Fern Appleby, grown matronly, affable as ever, and toting a granddaughter about the grounds. Before that, at a class reunion, I renewed acquaintances with several, including dream girl Martha Fisher still physically attractive despite having borne five kids—but that is all some ten years past.

This time, I was down for a funeral; meeting and talking with several persons, not of my generation, who never the less remembered me from my youth. I had attended mainly because my aged mother needed a driver—it was a cousin from a branch of her family (maternal side) whose members I hardly knew. The conversations took place at the obligatory coffee and lunch, after the graveside gathering, in the church basement.

At first, I stood apart, coffee cup in hand, letting my eyes scan the scene until a garrulous Gray Haired in his eighties accosted me, in a friendly fashion, and he advised me of his age immediately after introducing himself. Because I escorted mother and have some of her looks seemingly it was easy to pick me out. Uniformly, those with whom I talked seemed genuinely pleased to be chatting with Irene Sinclair's grown-up son.

For my part, I confess it was a rather pleasant experience although little more than revealing basic details of our lives, conversation soon drying up, and then drifting off to some other pairing and doing the same.

Mostly, I provided routine answers to routine questions about myself:

"Do you have a wife and family?"

"Yes."

"What is it you do?"

"Engineering."

Once this sort of conversation pretty well exhausted itself, I left mother to continue her visiting while I slipped down town on the pretext that there was something I had to see or do.

Few changes had taken place in Turnbull since my youth. What had once been Doc Rafferty's lot and shop was now a fairly modern looking Bank complex, Chang's old restaurant still offering refreshments, the site next had become a Government Liquor store now privatized and sharing space with a Bottle Depot Pop Shop which handled bottle returns, pop, used books and, so the sign said: Antiques and Confectionery. The old Village Office was no more, and the Drug Store had gotten a face-lift and looked quite modern in its new appearance. The rest of the business section looked well kept, still functioning more or less upon its original lines. The Banner, an exception, had relocated and sharing space on the off-street side of a forties radio and appliances store now operating as a pure water and health foods outlet. The Turnbull heart attack statistics running high as did the sodium content of the local water statistically, mating the two—death rate and water softness—thereby creating the perfect sales pitch for the product. Long time ethnic food habits and genetics never factored in to the equation.

In any case, I did not spend a lot of time wandering and was quite ready to return to the city once the reception had run its course. Even so, past events of my village life lingered on in my subconscious for several days; surfacing in idle moments both at the office and at home. Gradually such moments became less immediate and temporal, until the day of the annual Engineers versus Lawyers Winner's Cup and Grudge match.

In the scheme of things, it is an event not well known outside the two societies but it is none-the-less a championship game of sorts. And so into it, as my son would say. First off, I took a penalty for hip checking a fast and tricky winger in, I have to confess, a no-hit game. It was partly unintentional and partly opportune revenge on the Lawyers. You have to understand the nature of the beasts; as a body, Lawyers dislike losing. It's their nature. Engineers are just as determined to be winners and no less calculating. That being said, over time we learned that as a group they were quite willing to bend or ignore rules particularly when falling behind in the score. Such was the case during this annual match—Law Society versus Society of Engineers: losers buy the beer and finger food; winners get to gloat and gain possession of the prestigious 'Tin Finger Cup'—I leave it to the reader's imagination to determine what it looked like. Funny thing I do not remember whether we did win that year or not. What I do remember is that as I reached down to assist the winger, whom I had just knocked down, whilst mumbling mandatory but unfelt apologies, I heard a voice call out "Up to your old tricks Banger" or words to that effect. Surprised, I let go of the guy-corporate lawyer-causing him to hit the ice for a second time and turning polite acceptance of our collision into an indignant demand for a penalty call. I did not intend to drop him I was just so startled. Addressed as Banger was so unexpected, a nickname out of the past with hardly a soul who would knowingly call me that.

The moniker was a holdover from High School days and was tagged on me, a low scorer, for having once slap shoted a game winner all the way from the blue line, during a high school zone tournament. Forever after, I was called Banger this or that; but always it was said with good-humoured affection by my friends. At least that is my story, Johnny amongst others dispute the origins. At any rate, one more time, I reached to assist the unfortunate winger up off the ice before skating over to for a closer look at the man who had called out from behind the goalie mask. My first thought being that this guy might be another ringer as lawyers being lawyers may have researched this little tid-bit just to give them some obscure advantage.

I realize this all sounds very absurd but you would readily understand if you have ever competed against lawyers. They were not above parachuting in some ex-semi-pro to bolster their ranks. My suspicions, well founded, because just one year prior they brought in Red Macintyre, who had played for a short time in the old WHL. He single-handedly demolished our defense while centering a couple of not too bad wingers from the law firm of Macintyre, Macintyre, Jensen, and Associates. The lawyers figured because of the name our guy wouldn't question it. But he did. So then, they claim, that because Macintyre was helping out on a well-known criminal case involving a BC. Man, he qualified. In addition, this information, only after we discovered that J.C. (Red) Macintyre was not of the local firm Mcintyre, Macintyre, Jensen, and Associates. Mind you, in fairness, once, only once, we did have on our roster a young offensive defenseman—Hockey Scholarship McGill (Circa 1985). I must add, that unlike the Lawyers, our man was part of an International and affiliated firm with local offices here and elsewhere; practically one of the family I would say; and, I point out, we did it only after we had been twice duped out of a win. And was he good! Oh did the lawyers howl. Nevertheless, as I say, he was legitimate, in town trouble-shooting a major project at our request and with us for over a month's time.

This was why I did not clue in as to who the Law team's goalie actually was. Most of us don't bother to check over the team lists; leaving that as we do, to a designate. Quite simply, it was a case of "if you don't have a name you won't learn his name." An identity could not be made just by peering at a mask or sizing up a body type nor by checking out the guy's padding. All I knew about him was the fact that he was not the regular-net minder and that our guy had declared him eligible to play. However, I did have some sense of him being blocky and black-haired but that of itself did not ring any bells. Moreover, I had paid little attention to the man in front of the net partly because I played defense and we only had a very short pre-game warm-up; each to our own end for only about fifteen minutes before playing—evening ice-time being at a premium and not our regular rink time. Moreover, there was the fact that I did not know that Johnny was even in town. He was another corporate Lawyer a recent transferee in by his Company and it had been years and years since we had talked.

After the game, when the very frivolous formalities were over, excuses put forth and so on we had a chance to get together in an almost quiet corner. We talked for a time just setting out where our careers had taken us. To our mutual satisfaction we both were married and still to the same women we had started out with, each had children and a starting of grandchildren. Our conversation was mostly about those sorts of things that matter only to old acquaintances and are of little consequence to anyone else. Eventually the conversation became reminiscent and turned naturally to our early days in Turnbull. Johnny lost his father in '85 (heart) his mother now living with a daughter and aging gracefully, unlike my own mother who refuses to be treated like a person of her advanced years, sometimes scandalizing my young sister who had come unexpected and later in life. I fear she expects mother to behave like everyone's grandmother but in truth, the old dear does not. Talk drifted over to some of the Village characters we both knew. Such as the likes of Smith-Jones whose other-culture behaviour we never quite knew what to make of. This was in contrast to Johnny's father who was Chinese and so behaved in perfectly predictable if, as Johnny put it, "very Chinese ways." Smith-Jones, on the other hand, being English and culturally somewhat better matched, often appeared foreign to our notion of Canadian mores. In truth, his ordinary habits frequently surprised and sometimes baffled us. Language it seems in his case did not bridge the barriers of culture as one might have expected. I knew that he and Mrs. Smith-Jones—funny I do not to this day know what her first name was—had retired to Victoria some years past. Johnny and I instantly agreed that it was a fitting place for them. Gassing? Carl Gassing sold out one day and moved away to where I know not and I would guess he either is an incredibly old man or has long since passed away. He was good for the community and someday someone should recognize his community spirit—I loosely promised that I would look into it and perhaps do something. There were others: Captain Jack, for one, quietly passed away one day while tending his garden—a nice way to go I should think. Grandad Cade died when I was still a boy. I remember being surprised that a rather large number of citizens turned out for the funeral. Perhaps it was because he had been such a fiery preacher and citizen advocate that people were afraid if they didn't he would remember and meet them at the Gates when it was their turn. We talked for some time in this vein and naturally turned to the big game when the Turnbull Tigers almost became champions. It still seemed an important thing in our lives and we exchanged anecdotes for quite some time about the game itself and that period in our lives possibly because 1939 was such an historic time uprooting and affecting even those of us too young to engage in war.

Village life was never the same after that. Because most of the young able-bodied men of our town enlisted, many of us prematurely took on adult roles. The majority of enlistments from Turnbull took place during the early stages of war.

Several of our young men were never to come back. Leon Shultz—Dieppe: captured and died in a Concentration Camp and given a very hard time because of his German name, Dutch—real name Arthur—Jamieson lost on an air raid over Cologne, there were others who died in lesser know places including my cousin Busher MacLean whose death made war very personal. His father, my uncle, made me a present of his Winchester single shot, which I do not use but still have to this day. Of the survivors, Tucker Monroe being one, a few came back to Turnbull picked up their lives and went back to working in a family business or settled with the help of VLA—Veteran's Land Act—on to one of the district farms. I regret to add that one or two ended up like Sid Simpson—the Tigers' goalie with the hot hands—unable to make the transition from war to peace. It was rather sad watching the likes of Sid Simpson just kind of existing ever after never doing a great lot of anything. However, most did get on with their lives exceedingly well. One can certainly say that of Tucker Monroe.

Tucker, said by many, turned out to be a real get-up-and-goer. In Johnny's and my view, he always had been. Rough around the edges sometimes, despite or, as some would say because of, his genteel upbringing he took a veteran's loan and became a teacher and settled down in Turnbull from where he had started out. The thing most of us remember about Tucker was that after the big game was over, the Royals' management invited him to try out next season for the Edmonton Royals. Ourselves, and most of the villagers were proud of the fact that he had come up through our local hockey organization. Charlie Sayer wrote up a nice article in the Turnbull Banner, which I had the pleasure of re-reading whilst poking through old copies of the Banner. The current owners kindly brought them out for me to peruse helping me to verify many of the details in the events I have described in this writing. Of course, war intervened and he never got to play at that level. Who knows, Tucker might eventually have made NHL.

We did not finish talking on that occasion, in fact we found ourselves being almost the last to leave the Sports Lounge where we had been holding forth. We promised to get together over lunch at first opportunity and continue our reminiscences.

We were to meet again but not as soon as we thought; even so, the contact with Johnny Chang had opened a flood of remembering old times and events. My thoughts did not center on Turnbull exclusively but over the next few weeks remembrances would pop into my mind and I would catch myself daydreaming. Suddenly, some subtle signaller would turn my thoughts away from the specifications and mechanical details, of the particular project I was working on, to remembering some obscure hockey score from back in my youth that was important to me personally.

Dear to my heart still is the memory of scoring my first goal, a winner in a five to six Pee Wee hockey game over our fiercest rivals, The Clear View Pioneers. It was almost an accident but I cherish it anyhow. There was a pileup in front of the Pioneer net, their goalie dived out of the net grabbed at the puck, indeed everyone thought he had it in his glove hand, and waited expectantly for the referee to blow the whistle, the puck having been rendered out of play. Except that it wasn't, and only the referee and I saw that it was actually lying away from the left goal pad. The whistle might have gone, but, just as the referee caught up to the play, the puck dribbled onto clear ice between the spread-eagled legs of the goalie. The referee looked at me and I just reached down and pushed it in before I was knocked down in the pileup. Not the only goal I ever got; there were a few others, but I must add that then, rather than now, defense men mostly stuck to defending and except for power plays defense men were not looked to for their scoring power. Of course, exceptions always arise but I was never one of them. I guess one's first goal is a bit like one's first serious girl friend—neither is ever forgotten.

978-0-595-43029-1
0-595-43029-5

Printed in the United States
129943LV00001B/8/P

9 780595 430291